FINDING EVIE

A NOVEL

Catina Noble

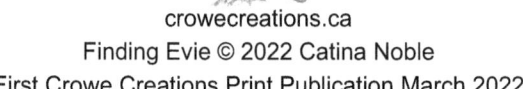

crowecreations.ca
Finding Evie © 2022 Catina Noble
First Crowe Creations Print Publication March 2022

This is a work of fiction based on the lives of children raised in homes with at least one parent having addiction issues and/or Narcissistic Personality Disorder. The patterns of abuse by addicts and/or those with NPD are so similar, any resemblance to persons living or dead is inevitable.

Front cover photo needpix.com
Cover Design © 2022 Crowe Creations
Interior design by Crowe Creations
Text set in Times New Roman; headings in Crazy Girlz Blond BTN

Crowe Creations ISBN: 978-1-927058-88-6

To my Aunt Judy, and my sisters, Valerie and Cori.

When parents tell their little kid, "It's all your fault," they're lying.

Preface

A<small>S THE COPYRIGHT PAGE STATES</small>: "This is a work of fiction based on the lives of children raised in homes with at least one parent having addiction issues and/or Narcissistic Personality Disorder. The patterns of abuse by addicts and/or those with NPD are so similar, any resemblance to persons living or dead is inevitable."

Some of this story was inspired by my own experiences, but it echoes the lives of all children, male and female, who grow up in less-than-perfect homes and may themselves, therefore, end up with addiction issues that will curse their own children. This book had to be written.

I'm hoping at least some of my readers will say, "Now I know why I hate myself so much. It isn't me. It's what was done to me. I have to stop the pattern." And others to say, "Wow. I was *this close* to having that happen to me. How lucky can a person be?"

CN
March 2022

1

I WAS SEVENTEEN. THINGS HAD BECOME steadily worse for me since my father had moved back in. You would think, after everything, he would have tried to make an effort. It was the complete opposite. It was as though he couldn't stand the sight of me or even handle being in the same room with me. I couldn't understand why.

My mother did nothing to help foster even a semblance of father–daughter relationship between us. I was tired of her pretending that nothing was going on, but I guess that was her way of coping. I do believe she feared him at times. But that did nothing to help me, or defeat my father's inevitable wrath. He would get annoyed with my two younger sisters, and even yell at them, but for some reason, I seemed to be the main focus of his anger and abuse.

My father was a short man, but taller than I was and he had lightning-fast speed. He was such a force, he could smack you and it would take you maybe five minutes to figure out what had just happened.

On this particular night, something was different. My father had been drinking yet again. I could see the rage building in his piercing blue eyes when they locked with mine. I don't know how to explain it because this kind of thing had been going on throughout my entire childhood., but something was off this time. I had to make a decision. And fast.

I honestly didn't have a plan for how I was going to get out of this particular situation, or how it might end, or whether this night might change anything, or if it might change everything. None of that mattered right then. I just knew something had to be done. Things weren't going to end well, that much I knew. I had this bad feeling.

I turned to my mother for support. Surely, she had to realize how dangerous the unfolding scene was.

"Mom, can't you see I need help? I can't take this anymore. It shouldn't be like this." There was no way she could just sit back and watch anymore. She had to do *something*.

She was sitting at the kitchen table. She was wearing her pale-blue, long-sleeved nightgown with the zipper down the front and she was working on one of her word search games or crossword puzzles. She didn't react in the slightest at the sound of my voice. It was as though she were trying to ignore me, and everything else that was going on.

This time, I wasn't going to let her do that.

"Mom. I know you can hear me. Turn around."

She turned and her eyes met mine. She spoke quietly. "Evie, you know better than to upset your father. You know better than that."

The thing was, I hadn't done anything. It was the same as it always was. I was being punished for something I hadn't done. My father hated me for things I didn't do. There was something wrong with him. He needed help.

How could she even think for a moment this was my fault? She was sitting not even six feet away from us. I was the kid here. They were the parents. Did they not have some sort of obligation? They weren't doing what they were supposed to be doing. I tried to recall the last time I had seen my father this upset. I couldn't.

All I had wanted to do was sleep at a friend's place because Dad was completely drunk. My sisters had already gone to spend a night with their friends. I didn't want to be his punching bag. That's what it basically boiled down to. He seemed to be on a fresh wave of rage. I thought I might vomit. I glanced at the back screen door where my friend PJ stood waiting, just outside. She was fifteen. I'm sure she could hear every word. I had no time to be embarrassed about what she might hear. I would worry about that later. Right then, I had to keep my wits about me.

My father had noticed my eyes looking toward the door. He took another swig from his Molson Canadian beer—I can still picture that bottle—and through his gritted teeth he spoke.

"I'll give you one warning and only one." He pointed his beer bottle at me. "You try leaving this house and I will slice your fucking throat."

I could feel my eyes bulging. This was not happening. This wasn't real. I looked over in my mother's direction once more, my eyes pleading for help. She never even looked up. She continued sitting there, immersed in her all-important puzzle.

My father sucked down the last of the beer then smashed the bottle against the door jamb. His hand reached down to the shards of it and taking the biggest piece, he lunged at me.

I ran for my life.

PJ was right there with me and together we ran to her place. My parents knew that she and I were friends, but they didn't know she lived in the same neighborhood, two buildings over from us.

PJ's mother was super sick and had been for months. I had visited PJ several times and every time I was there, her mother was in bed, too sick to come out. (And no, her mom wasn't a drug addict like many parents in our neighborhood were.) Once we got to her place, PJ explained what had happened and I was told that I was welcome to stay at their place for as long as need be.

Half an hour after arriving at PJ's, I heard the phone ring. PJ answered. It was my mother. She wanted to talk to me. I refused.

There was nothing my mother could say to convince me to come home. I didn't want to hear anything. I needed space. There was a lot to process. My father had just threatened to kill me. My father had come after me with a chunk of broken beer bottle to slice my throat. My mother had sat there ignoring the entire thing. Was this another of my nightmares?

"No," PJ had assured me.

Had I asked that out loud? No. I wasn't going crazy. PJ had been there. PJ had heard everything.

So this was all really happening.

My mother informed PJ that if I weren't home in the next fifteen minutes, she was going to call the police. My own mother was going to call the police on me!

I decided it was not in my best interests to go home. So I didn't.

2

M Y SISTERS RETURNED THE NEXT day from their sleepovers and, I learned later, had been shocked to find out I'd run away from home.

I felt bad that I hadn't taken them with me, but I had no way of supporting them. I was even worried that if I tried to meet up with them for lunch, my parents would call the police and try to have me arrested for kidnapping or something. I couldn't trust my parents at all. The best thing for everyone was to have some time apart.

I stayed with PJ for a few days and then went to another friend's place to stay. I returned home after a week to pick up my stuff. It was obvious to me I wasn't moving back home, and my parents never tried to convince me any different. At this point, I would rather have died on the streets than go back.

My mother was home when I arrived to pick up my stuff but, to my relief, my father was out. My sisters weren't around either. I think my mother had sent them away on purpose to make sure they didn't create a scene. (Or witness anything?) It was probably better that way because I had no idea what I would do if my sisters had started begging me to stay.

I decided to pack as much stuff as I could carry as I had to take a bus back to where I was staying. It turned out there was no need to worry about having too much to carry. My mother was not letting me take a whole lot. I was allowed to take a few outfits and personal items, and that was it. The rest was staying, she told me, because it was her house and everything was under her roof.

3

I HAD ALWAYS PICTURED MYSELF, PERHAPS in my late twenties, getting married to my one true love. We would live in a cute little house, share a car, have at least two kids—a boy and a girl, of course. My husband and I might even have a cat and a dog and a white picket fence. We would take family vacations once a year and maybe, one day, I would be able to take a trip on my own.

Imagine me, out having my own adventures.

My mother once admitted to me that she'd wanted out of her family home, so she'd lied to my father about being pregnant so he would marry her.

"Did he propose then?" I asked.

They were on a picnic, she told me, and they got into a fight and he threw the ring at her.

Not exactly a great foundation for a relationship, was it?

My parents, Gabe and Molly, were married by a Justice of the Peace. A few close friends and family members attended and Mom's mother, Gram, put on the reception at her place.

My father was nineteen, and my mother was eighteen.

My mother was eighteen when she had me. By the time she was twenty-four, she'd had three of us, all girls.

Want to hear something funny? I almost ended up with a different set of parents altogether. And I often wondered how differently my life might have turned out. Of course, there's always the flip side. I could have had it worse. But somehow, I doubt that. Maybe I would have been an only child. Maybe my parents would have been ready to be parents. Maybe I would have had parents who actually wanted me, loved me. I still wonder what it would have felt like to be loved by parents.

This is what happened.

My mother had a difficult time during my delivery, so she was given extra medication that overwhelmed her. On top of that, I expelled my meconium, my baby feces, so I needed extra attention and recovery time, too.

When my mother was feeling better, she asked the nurse, "Would you please bring me my baby? I want to hold her and really see her."

"Sure, Mrs. Feathers. I'll be back in a minute."

Ten minutes later, the nurse returned with a baby all snuggled up in a hospital blanket.

"Here you go. Here is your beautiful baby. I'll stay for a moment then leave you two alone so you can get acquainted. If you need anything, just let me know."

My mother took the baby in her arms then laid the bundle on her hospital bed.

The nurse smiled. "What did you name him, Mrs. Feathers? Or have you decided yet?"

"We're going to call her— Wait! A him? What are you talking about? I had a girl."

"Are you sure, Mrs. Feathers? You did have a lot of painkillers. Maybe you're confused?"

"No. I had a girl. A baby girl. They told me. I had a baby girl. She weighs seven pounds, eleven ounces. Where the hell is my baby?"

"Mrs. Feathers. I am so sorry. Give me the baby back and I'll go check the nursery. I'll see what's going on."

Another ten minutes passed until a different nurse returned with me, all bundled up in a blanket.

My mother quickly took me into her arms and laid me down on the bed to check me over from head to toe, double checking the hospital bracelet attached to my leg: Baby Girl Feathers. 7-11. They'd gotten it right this time.

The other nurse was new, they told her, in a rush, so had grabbed the baby beside me by mistake.

Another glint of hope that I had the wrong parents came up again.

As part of a school project, one day, every student in the class had to bring in their baby books. My parents brought out mine and both my sisters' baby books, but mine was literally just the outside of the book with not a single page inside. That was mostly how I felt about myself most of the time when I was at home. Just the cover. Nobody inside. I could have said that as a joke when I saw the book like that, except there was nothing funny about it. Nothing at all. Was that why my parents didn't love me? They didn't see that somebody was supposed to be in here?

I asked them what had happened and they said they "weren't sure."

Weren't parents supposed to keep important baby items? How careless of them.

How embarrassing for me when I was doing my presentation with just the cover of my baby book and nothing else. When I was finished talking, my classmates, who were allowed to ask me questions, began.

"What happened to the insides?" one of them asked.

Another told me it was OK. It just meant I was probably adopted.

News to me, but it might explain my parents' attitude.

I decided that this idea of my being adopted was something I should take a closer look into. Silly me for not coming to this conclusion on my own earlier.

The adoption theory stayed with me for two years. I kept asking my parents questions while wondering how to go on the quest to find my real parents.

Whenever we saw other family members, I would ask them questions. Had they seen me in the hospital when I was born. Had my mother looked pregnant. Did they know anything about my birth. I interviewed relatives and went over hospital records but found no proof that I was adopted. The only thing I did end up with was more frustration and more of the same old questions. Why had my parents hated me so much? What did I do wrong?

Years later, through some of my psych courses, I learned that most children go through this phase, wondering if they were adopted or not. I knew, of course, that I had not been adopted but even to this day, there's that subconscious hope that I was, that I hadn't inherited my parents' genes. Hope lives eternal, doesn't it? I think hope is what keeps us alive sometimes.

4

A S A CHILD, I WAS led to believe that the main role of parents consisted of two things, and only two: if you have a roof over your head, you're lucky; if you have food once in a while, you're truly lucky.

I use the phrase "once in a while" regarding food because I was often hungry. My parents would not allow us to just go to the fridge or cupboard and take food when we wanted to. (A secret here: so I "stole" it.)

A good part of the time, my parents weren't even home to cook, or to eat with us. They would have gone to the neighborhood bar, or they'd eat at the mall where my mother worked. I'd be at home with my sisters, waiting and wondering what we were going to have for supper.

When they got home, I would ask and they would snap at me, letting me know that they had eaten and we should make the meal ourselves.

The problem was, though, there was rarely ever any food in the house. My parents would grocery-shop maybe once a month, and it wasn't a big one. They would buy a case of twenty-four pop. I would have one can. A few days later, my mother or my father would go to get a can and there would be none and they would be absolutely furious. They would scream and yell, demanding to know where all the pop and food had gone. With twenty-four cans of pop and five people, it would last perhaps a week? My parents would buy three small boxes of cereal and expect that to last us three girls an entire month. One box would last three days at the most. We never had a second bowl either because that wasn't allowed.

There were times I sold things from around the house or from my room just to get money so I could buy food. I sold my keyboard, a ring that my mother had given me, saying it was costume jewelry (turns out it wasn't), and two coins from my father's coin collection. (My mother sold the rest of his collection later on.) My parents never seemed to notice the missing items. Was that because it was always small things? I think they must have wondered where my keyboard had gone, but never asked. How did I sell these things? An older friend took the items to a pawn shop.

It should not have been like this.

When I was older, one of my high-school friends told me she knew how things were at my place. Every so often, we would go to her house for lunch. We would eat there, and she would fill up my school bag to the brim with snacks and things I could eat without having to cook it. That way, when I or my sisters were hungry, I could give them something small so my parents wouldn't catch on. I knew if my parents found out that someone outside the family knew they didn't always feed us, that they controlled the food, that they ate out all the time, there would have been hell to pay.

I know now that children need a lot more than just food and a roof. But I didn't know any better back then. I thought we were just a normal family. The older I got, the more I realized that my family *wasn't* a typical one, that my sisters and I deserved much better. I just didn't know where to turn. It seemed that whenever I tried to reach out to *get* help, it never worked. I was either disappointed with the result, or worse, I ended up being punished by my parents.

I'm still full of envy when I hear people talking about their favorite childhood memories. Friends will talk about the many birthdays and Christmases and traditions and events they were able to enjoy while growing up. During my younger years, I pretended to know what everyone was talking about. Now, I know that not all parents provide the basic necessities for their children and mine fell into that category.

That understanding hasn't stopped me from struggling with the subconscious belief that my parents didn't love me because something was wrong with me, or that they kept me around only so I could look after my sisters, be a slave to my parents.

It's healthy for kids to have chores, of course it is, but not to be the maid and nanny for everyone in the house. I was not your parent. You were mine. At least, you were supposed to be.

5

I'M FOUR OR FIVE YEARS old. My stomach is growling but I know it's not time to get up yet because my room is dark. I'm hungry and I'm thirsty. I try to fall back to sleep to make the time go by faster but I can't; and I want the darkness to go away so it will be time to eat breakfast, but that's not happening either. My stomach keeps growling and I know from experience that crying makes it worse. Crying makes me hungrier and thirstier, makes my stomach growl more and more.

I sit up in bed and listen. I don't hear my mother or my father walking around or talking. I think maybe they're sleeping. I'm scared. What will happen if they catch me?

I decide to try anyway and I slowly climb out of my bed. I peel back my bedroom door. It's on carpet so it doesn't make a sound. I check the hallway. I don't see anyone. The tiny light in the kitchen that my mother always leaves on, does nothing, but it's not as dark as my bedroom. I am wearing nothing but my pink underwear.

I tiptoe quietly along the carpeted hallway as I make my way toward the kitchen. I want to run. I want to get everything over with. But I can't do that. My parents always tell me I sound like an elephant when I run. I need to keep quiet no matter what.

I glance around the kitchen but I don't see any food anywhere. I don't know what I was expecting but although I'm disappointed, I'm not ready to give up just yet.

My eyes travel the counter back and forth again.

I finally see something. It's not much, and I would have preferred a slice of bread, but it's something.

It's the sugar my parents keep on the counter to put in their coffee. The jar is filled with sparkly white stuff. It looks kind of pretty.

I stretch out my hand to grab the sugar jar. I can't reach it. I get up on my tiptoes as far as I can, hold my breath, and stretch out my hand as far as it will go but I still can't reach the jar. I need to be taller.

I grab a kitchen chair and glide it over slowly, carefully, quietly to the counter. I climb the chair and almost clap my hands together with excitement but I must not make any noise.

I did it.

I pull the jar toward me and take off the top. I try to grab a handful of sugar but it slips through my fingers like water. I need to figure out a way to get it into my mouth. I lick my right pointing finger and dip it into the sugar. I pull it out. Sugar is now stuck to my finger. I lick it off. I dip it back in again, and again. I would have kept dipping and licking the sugar, but the thought returns that I'm not supposed to be doing this. That I will be in big trouble if I get caught. I need to get back to my room. Right now.

I dip my finger one last time. Then I need to make sure I lick it all off. If I can't see it, then my mother and father won't be able to see it either. I won't get into trouble. I don't want a spanking. Spankings hurt.

I can't get the lid back on the jar like it was before.

My hands are shaking.

I need to get back to my room.

The light in the kitchen suddenly becomes brighter.

I panic and drop the sugar jar. It falls to smash on the floor and launch sugar everywhere. There's sugar on the counter, the floor, the chair. I nearly fall to the floor myself, and would have, except for my mother who's grabbing me hard on my not-for-writing hand. She snatches me off the chair.

"Ow!" I try to wriggle away from her. She doesn't let go. I'm stuck.

"What do you think you're doing, brat?"

"I'm hungry. My stomach's growling and I want it to stop." By now, I'm crying. "I just want it to stop so I can sleep."

She drags me down the hallway to my bedroom doorway.

"Get into your bed right now. Don't make another sound and do not leave your room for any reason. If you do, you will be very sorry. I will deal with you in the morning."

She shoved me into my room and shut the door.

I climbed back into my bed, pulled my pillow close to me and sobbed into it. I didn't dare risk getting into trouble for making more noise. I was in enough trouble already. The worst part was not that I was in trouble—I was used to that—but I was still hungry and thirsty, and my stomach was still growling.

I did get into a lot of trouble for what my parents started calling The Stunt. That morning, I was not allowed to have breakfast. I was spanked and had to stay in my room the entire day, alone.

They let me use the bathroom, and I was allowed supper that evening, but that was it.

They got themselves a new sugar jar but never again left it out on the counter. The counter remained bare of anything to eat for as long as I can remember. Probably the cupboards, too, but I was too small, and too scared, to get up there to look.

I have since learned that if we have no love when we are growing up, we often substitute it with something else, like food, or drink. I guess that's the reason I felt like I was always starving to death.

6

OVER THE COURSE OF MY entire kindergarten era, I would get into trouble because of "stunts" I apparently pulled. Two particular incidents come to mind and both confused me because I did what I was told, but then I was the one who got in trouble.

Back in my day, we had Show and Tell every Friday. I loved Show and Tell. All the kids brought something both fun and interesting to show to the entire class.

On this particular Show and Tell day, I was excited. Usually, I just brought in silly stuff from my bedroom because I didn't have anything fun and interesting. At one time, I'd had a couple of awesome jigsaw puzzles, but I had left one of them out around the time my little sister, Dee Dee, had started crawling. She found the puzzle, destroyed it, and even ate some of the pieces.

I told on her, but it didn't matter because I was the one who was in trouble. I "should have known better" than to leave puzzle pieces on the floor. Dee Dee "didn't know not to touch them because she's so young."

My parents threw my other jigsaw puzzles in the garbage, too.

Being the eldest is no fun. I stand by this statement and will forever. My mother was the youngest in her family and my father was somewhere in the middle of his. Any kid born after the first one, learns by example from his siblings and often through what happens to his older siblings what and, especially, what *not* to do. My parents had plenty of tutors. I had none. Was that why my parents "assumed" I should always know better? Did they think kids were born knowing? Other kids I knew who were the eldest in their families were tutored by their own parents. They were taken aside and patiently taught what was right and what was not right. Not so for me. My parents must have believed they were born knowing the rules. They weren't. And neither was I.

Show and Tell was going to be different this time. I had something special to bring in to show everyone.

The night before that class, I had seen my father drawing and coloring. He seemed quiet and happy when he was doing it, so I sat there, quietly watching him, enjoying this very different moment. I kept waiting for him to yell at me, as usual, to tell me to go find something to do, or go help my mother, but he didn't. He just kept sketching, erasing the odd line here and there, and every so often he'd pick up a coloring pencil and swipe it across the page. The picture got prettier and prettier as he added more colors. I was impressed.

I couldn't wait to go to school the next day and tell everyone my father performed magic. The kids in my class would want to be friends with me for sure! As far as I knew, none of my classmates knew a magician. Maybe I would finally get invited to someone's birthday party.

With a serious look, my father handed me his pack of twenty-four coloring pencils. Usually, when my father's face was serious like this, I was about to get in trouble for something, but this time would be different.

"I mean it. Don't let anyone touch or use these pencils." My father always ordered, never tutored. "You can pass them around to show them off, but no one is to use them. And this means you, too. These are my special pencils. I need them for sketching."

I couldn't help but smile. I couldn't wait to show them off.

"Well, Evie? Did you hear me?"

"Yes. No one uses these pencils. Not even me. They are your special pencils. Just for you to use."

Of course, I wasn't going to let anyone use the pencils. I mean, really, who did he think I was?

On the other hand, how the heck would he know if I used them? Would he actually measure the pencils when I got home to make sure no one had used them?

***

Once at school, I could barely contain my excitement. I tried to focus on the different things we were doing, but all I wanted was to get into the circle and get ready for Show and Tell.

Finally, it was time! Everyone in the class sat in a circle on the carpet. We all quieted down. Mrs. Sadie would never start Show and Tell until everyone was seated in a circle and we were all quiet. Sometimes, this felt like forever.

I think some of the kids didn't understand what the word "quiet" actually meant. I was good at it. Very good. Especially at home. Or when my parents and I went out somewhere. My father would always question me.

"What are the two most important rules we need to follow, absolutely, no matter what, when we are outside in public? Do you know them, Evie?"

"Children should be seen but not heard. I am not supposed to talk unless someone talks to me. The second rule is not to pull any stunts."

I was very aware of the first rule. I'd been well trained at home to keep my mouth shut.

I tried to follow the second one as well even though I didn't really understand it. I mean, it's not like I decided to get in trouble on purpose. Who would do that when you knew you'd most likely get a beating for it, or have your toys taken away? It seemed that the rules were always changing and I was the only one who had to follow them. I was four years old. None of the adults had to follow any rules. (Especially my parents.) And my sister Dee Dee didn't have to follow any rules, either. She was a baby. None of the kids I knew had to follow rules. Just me. Even at that age, I resented it.

Mrs. Sadie brought her pointer finger to her lips. This was a good sign. It meant that at any moment she was going to ask us who wanted to go first. We would all put our hands up at the same time then she would keep us in suspense by calling out our names, one at a time, until each of us had presented something for Show and Tell.

I tried to raise my hand higher than I usually did, and I put on my best smile. My efforts didn't seem to matter to Mrs. Sadie. She didn't call my name until there was only one other kid besides me left. Christopher. Next time, I told myself, I won't volunteer at all, and she'll pick me on purpose, thinking I'm not ready.

Little did Mrs. Sadie know that I was on to her antics. I was starting to get good at knowing the antics of adults. I was a kid, but I'd had a lot of experience. Hadn't I?

7

WHEN MY TURN CAME, I presented my father's coloring pencils with a smile and made sure I displayed the pencils high up in the air, right above my head. I even pulled out two of my favorite colors, turquoise and purple. I must have done a pretty good job because Mrs. Sadie smiled at me and that was something she didn't do very often. I was very proud of myself. I watched nervously as my father's box of pencils went around the circle so everyone could get a good look at them. I was relieved that no one tried to open the box or throw it at the next person. I was feeling pretty good about how my presentation had turned out. I mean, if Mrs. Sadie was proud, I was proud.

After Show and Tell, we always went back to our desks to work on things. With a regular pencil, I was tracing more letters from my name inside the balloons the clown was holding. I already knew how to spell my name using the dotted lines for help but most of the class didn't. My parents had spent the entire summer before I started kindergarten getting me to trace my name over and over so I would know how to spell it by the time I started. This wasn't actually to help me. My father wanted to make sure no one thought that I, his child, was stupid. Despite my father's motives, this gave me extra confidence when I started class. Spelling my own name was something I was good at, and I knew it.

By this time, Mrs. Sadie was at her desk flipping papers back and forth. It was Miss Jane who was making the rounds. Miss Jane was the teacher's assistant.

As she passed by each of us, and looked down at our work, she would give a comment to each child. Soon, she was standing right beside me, watching.

"Great job, Evie. Are you going to color in your picture? It looks great, but if you add some color to the picture, it would look even better, don't you think?"

Miss Jane was right. As I looked around, I noticed all the other kids were busy coloring the clowns on their paper. I had already printed all the letters in my name, one inside each of the balloons. There was really nothing left to do except color the clown holding the balloons. I also knew that when Miss Jane "suggested" something, it meant you were supposed to do it even though she always made it sound like it was actually your idea and not hers. I liked that about her. And I was having a good day at school, and recently, with life in general, so I wanted to make sure I kept it that way.

"Okay," I said as I reached into my desk to pull out my box of crayons. I would start with the color purple and then go from there.

"Why don't you use the pretty coloring pencils you showed us at Show and Tell? It would make your picture look nice."

Why would she even mention that? We always used crayons for everything. If we were going to use something else, then Mrs. Sadie told us, and we got into groups, and shared the materials she wanted us to use. She hadn't done that so that meant we were to use our own crayons for work. I looked around at the rest of the class. Every single child was using their own set of crayons.

I shook my head no. I wasn't going to use my father's pencils. I mean, sure, I'd thought about it. It would be exciting and bad all at once. But I was a smart cookie. I knew that somehow my father would find out I had not listened to him and had used the coloring pencils. I would be in so much trouble for pulling another "stunt" and my father had seemed really happy when he was using his pencils. When my father was happy, he wasn't yelling or being mean to me. My father needed those pencils. I needed to keep those safe.

"No. These are my father's special pencils. No one is allowed to use them. Only he is allowed."

The explanation seemed straightforward to me: no one was to touch the coloring pencils. My father had explained it to me. I understood it. I explained it to Miss Jane so she could understand it as well. I had mentioned this in my presentation. My instructions were clear to everyone. Unfortunately, this would not be the case.

To my sheer horror, Miss Jane picked up the cherry-red coloring pencil.

She slowly crouched down and was now at my level.

She actually had the nerve to look directly at me before she put the pencil on the paper and started coloring the clown's nose.

She was using my father's pencils! I was going to get into so much trouble for this. Oh my gosh! It was one thing to get into trouble for something I did, like use the coloring pencils myself, but to get into trouble for something someone else did? Like Miss Jane using the pencils? That would be tragic and unfair.

I had to stop her.

"Don't touch them! I told you. No one's allowed to touch them. You did it on purpose." I was furious.

I tried grabbing the pencil out of her hand, but she had anticipated my move and stood up quickly, moving out of my reach.

I got up from my seat.

By now the whole class was watching us.

Mrs. Sadie looked over in our direction and asked what was going on.

I tried to explain to her what had happened while trying to contain my tears. It wasn't easy. The last thing I wanted to do was to start crying and have everyone in the class label me as a baby.

"I told Miss Jane not to touch the pencils. They are my father's pencils and no one is allowed to use them. I'm not even allowed to use them. She knows and did it anyway. Miss Jane did it on purpose." I folded my arms in front of me and waited for justice to be meted out.

Now it was time for Miss Jane to tell her side of the story. Maybe Miss Jane would get sent out to the hallway, or better yet, sent down to the principal's office. That would serve her right. Whatever happened to Miss Jane, she deserved it after what she'd done.

"I was trying help Evie with her work and then all of a sudden she tried to grab the pencil from me. I don't know what's wrong with her."

How the heck could she say she was trying to help me when she was actually stealing my stuff? Not my stuff, my father's stuff. What right did she have to even touch my paper? I hadn't given her permission. Every kid knew that you never touched another person's artwork or homework. Ever. It was just the way things were. Another rule I learned at school. There were so many rules to follow, it was exhausting at times. But I knew them.

"This is no way to behave at school, Evie. You know better than that. It wasn't very nice of you. Miss Jane was only trying to help you with your work. Not only have you upset Miss Jane, but you have disrupted the entire class. I can't have this going on in my classroom. It's not fair to the other children. I believe you need a time out so you can think about how rude you were to Miss Jane. How you overreacted and how disruptive you were to your classmates. Please go out to the hallway right now. When I think you have calmed down and might be ready to join the class, I will come and get you. Before you can come back to class, you will have to apologize to Miss Jane for your rude behavior. You will also have to apologize to the class."

Mrs. Sadie stretched out her right arm and pointed at the classroom door.

I started toward the door but turned back to collect my father's pencils. I didn't want anything else to happen to them. I was in enough trouble already.

"Evie! I said, out in the hallway. That means right this minute. It doesn't mean you can dilly-dally and do whatever you want first. You need to learn to listen."

"But I just want to put the pencils away so nothing happens to them."

"Go."

I wasn't trying to be difficult. I was trying to be responsible and do the right thing. How could she not see that?

By now, my tears were streaming. I made my way out into the hallway. I was embarrassed. Ashamed. My mother and father were going to be upset with me yet again. They would blame me, of course. No way they'd believe it was a teacher's fault. I probably wouldn't believe me, either, but it was the truth. I was always told to tell the truth no matter what. That was a rule, even though, in my house, my parents seemed to ignore that one most of the time. Maybe rules only applied to certain people? It was hard to keep it all straight sometimes.

***

I'm not sure how long I stayed out in the hallway. I was too young to tell time. I figured I was handling the situation, though. That is, until the principal spotted me and came over to talk.

He asked what I was doing outside the classroom. I mean, he knew. The only reason a student would be standing still in the hallway by herself was because she had gotten into trouble and had been sent out there by a teacher.

Maybe the principal was trying to test me. Maybe I could lie and tell him I was going to the washroom? That I forgot where it was?

No, that wouldn't work.

Look at me. Too young to tell time yet, but there I was scheming to deceive the principal. Just goes to show you the direction my "*home schooling*" was geared toward, doesn't it? And I wasn't even aware I had been learning to deceive. I wasn't even aware of who I was yet. But I certainly knew ways to get out of a rage-filled scolding, not that I was ever successful at it.

The principal asked me to tell me my side of the story.

Would it make a difference if I did? Not in my experience. In my experience, I was first wrong, secondly punished, then everything was forgotten about. Except by me.

I didn't want to be talking to the principal. Principals didn't talk to students. They didn't make time for them unless they were in trouble. The only time you saw a principal was at a school function. That was it. I did not want to be *seen* talking to the principal. My reputation would be ruined. I'd be labeled a bad kid for something I hadn't done. Enough of that happened at home. I didn't need it in front of my class-mates, too. Did I? I needed to be invisible like I had learned how to do at home.

But I talked to him. I had no choice, did I? I told him my side of the story then he told me to go back into the classroom and do whatever the teacher told me to do.

The first thing I did when I entered the room was head for my desk so I could put away my father's pencils. But Mrs. Sadie stopped me. I had to come up to the front of the class. How embarrassing. How humiliating. And I had done nothing wrong. I had been doing what my father had told me to do: don't let anybody touch his pencils.

To my classmates I said, "I'm sorry for my behavior and for disturbing everybody."

Then I apologized to Miss Jane. She didn't have to apologize to me.

Finally, I was allowed to go back to my desk to tidy up my stuff. It was almost home time.

To my horror, the cherry-red pencil Miss Jane had used to color in the clown's nose had been snapped in half.

I grabbed the two pieces of pencil, one in each hand. I looked up at Miss Jane who had her arms folded across her chest. She flashed me a pearly white smile. I honestly just wanted to walk over and kick her in the kneecaps, then make *her* go to the front of the class and apologize to everyone for *her* behavior. Wouldn't that have been something? How come *she* wasn't getting punished? I think she should have been sent out into the hallway to talk to the principal, too. It was her fault, not mine.

From then on, I hated Miss Jane.

Until that incident at school, I had loved kindergarten. I had felt grown up going to school every day with my knapsack, and telling everyone about my day when I got home. If no one at home asked, which was the usual, at least I got to tell my imaginary friends. They were always around.

I had lost trust in school. School was supposed to teach you right from wrong. You were supposed to learn important lessons you'd need later on in life. All I had learned was that life isn't fair, that it didn't matter if you were right or wrong. Where was the logic? After that incident, I still tried my best when it came to schoolwork, but my heart was never again in it. I had lost a part of myself.

That night, the moment my father set his eyes on me, I started bawling my eyes out. Even if the principal hadn't told him about the incident, he would know now that something was up. Either way, I was in trouble for sure. Back then, I wasn't much good at covering up my feelings. As the years went by, I got better and better at hiding the truth. Essentially hiding myself inside myself.

Wait until my father found out I had to stand out in the hallway where everyone could see that I was a bad kid. Would he keel over in shock when he found out that the principal had to come and speak to me? I mean, what kind of kid was I?

Even if the school hadn't called my father, I couldn't cover up my story. I had the broken pencil as evidence of my betrayal.

I was finally able to calm down enough to tell him what had happened at school, with Show and Tell, and about how my classmates had liked his beautiful coloring pencils. How we were coloring the clown after Show and Tell. I told him about Miss Jane and what she had done *with* his pencil then later, *to* his pencil. I showed him the broken cherry-red pencil as evidence that this whole thing was Miss Jane's fault.

Then I waited for my punishment. I'd be at least grounded. There was a chance he would even give me a spanking to go along with it and none of it was my fault. Miss Jane would get away with everything. I left out the part about having to stand up in front of the class and say sorry for my behavior, though. I just couldn't bring myself to tell him *that*. I had lived through that humiliating experience once and I didn't ever want to do it again, even in the telling. Besides, I could get punished for that as well. I had told my father *almost* everything, so decided that was good enough.

I was waiting for the blows to start, but I'd gotten lucky that day. For some reason, my father was in a good mood. Not only did my father not punish me, but he even allowed me to keep the coloring pencils.

Looking back at that incident, the word I would use to describe how my father had reacted to my story of the coloring pencils, was that he seemed "proud" of me. It felt good but it was a feeling I would experience only a handful of times during my entire childhood, so I would come to crave it.

I kept the pencils in my room. I loved those pencils and used them until they were too tiny to use anymore and even then, I just kept them. I never brought them to school again.

After that particular incident, Miss Jane's "stunt," I hated Show and Tell. Most of the time, I didn't bring anything to show, on purpose. I would tell Mrs. Sadie that I forgot. (I also tried to avoid Miss Jane as much as possible.)

Once I realized that each time you passed a grade you got another teacher, I was anxious to finish kindergarten and move on to Grade 1 where, hopefully, my new teacher would like me. Maybe, with luck, she would make sure everyone in the entire class followed the rules.

8

I GOT MY FIRST PET TURTLE when I was in kindergarten. I was excited. This would be my pet and my responsibility.

I don't remember where we got him from, if I even knew in the first place, but I named him Herman and I spent hours and hours watching him.

Once at Show and Tell, one of my classmates said I should bring Herman in and talk about him. That would be neat because no one in the class had a pet turtle. I thought about it. It would have been nice to let him walk around my desk while the other kids watched in envy and told me over and over again how lucky I was to have my very own turtle. The excitement built.

But then I remembered the incident with Miss Jane. There was no way I was going to bring Herman to school. Miss Jane would not be getting anywhere near my pet turtle. She would kill him on purpose and blame it on me. My job was to protect Herman. That meant he could never come to school with me.

I remember Herman lounging around in the bathroom as I got ready for school, and I put him beside me on the floor when I was eating breakfast. He was great company, and my parents didn't mind.

One day when I was at school, my mother found Herman dead on the bathroom floor. Maybe I'd handled him too much. I didn't know, but something had happened and he was dead.

That afternoon, when I got home from school, my mother sat me down. This was going to be "a chat," so I knew it wasn't going to be good. I was old enough, and experienced enough by then, to know that whenever any adult said they wanted to "talk to you for a minute," it was *never* good news. It was *always* bad.

"Remember we talked about how you were in charge of Herman? That he was your responsibility?" She was staring intently at me.

"Yes. He's my pet. He's my responsibility. And I think it's time to feed him."

"Just a second. I need to tell you something." She sounded serious.

"Okay. What?"

"Herman? The turtle? Well. He's gone. I'm sorry."

"Oh. Okay. I'll go find him. I need to feed him anyway." I hopped off my chair and headed for my room.

My mother trailed behind me. She stood there watching me search my room. I had no luck finding Herman. I sat down on my bed to think about where Herman could be hiding. He was so small, there could be many places. This could take me all night. But I was up for the challenge. Herman was my responsibility, so I didn't mind.

"Evie, I told you he isn't here."

"I know he's not here. That's why we need to find him."

I guess my mother didn't want to tell me the truth so she took another approach.

"Herman ran away. You won't find him in the house. You can look everywhere, but you will not find him. He's gone and you need to just accept it."

She crossed her arms. This was her sign. She was done talking and there would be no further discussion. The conversation was over and if I brought it up again, I would be in trouble.

I knew that, of course, but that didn't matter. I wasn't finished talking about Herman. I didn't care how much trouble I would be in, or even if I got a spanking out of this. Herman was worth it. I needed to do my best to get the bottom of whatever was going on. My parents would never get me another turtle if I lost Herman, but the main thing was, Herman was my best friend. I couldn't picture my life without him.

"Herman was happy," I told her. "He would never run away. A person or an animal would never run away if they're happy. They only run away when they're not happy." I tried to explain this to her. I shouldn't have had to. She was the parent. She should know this stuff already.

"Herman probably ran away because you didn't look after him properly."

I shook my head. "No. That's not true. I loved him. I took care of him. I always took care of him."

I wasn't buying her story at all. But somehow, I felt guilty. What if Herman *had* run away from me because I hadn't treated him well? Maybe she was telling me the truth. Maybe I was not responsible enough to have a pet of my own.

My mother said nothing more and left my room.

I was heartbroken. I tried a protest like they do on TV. The kind where people go on a hunger strike to get their point across. I refused supper but all that did was get me a smack on the back of the head and a "Smarten up!" Besides, when I didn't have enough food in it, my stomach would feel awful. I wouldn't be able to sleep if I didn't eat my supper.

My protest was short-lived. I ended up eating.

9

NOT LONG AFTER THE HERMAN incident with my mother, someone knocked at our door. I looked up from the TV but didn't move, of course. One of my parents always answered the door. "You never know who it could be so it's safer that way." This made sense to me, especially since I was uncomfortable around adults. I'd go with that rule with no complaints.

My mother yelled at me from the kitchen. "Evie. I'm doing the dishes. Answer the door. Don't forget to ask who it is first."

This sounded simple enough. I didn't think I could mess this up. I felt big and important as I walked over to the door.

"*WHO IS IT?*" I yelled at the top of my lungs. If my father had been home, he would have given me a slap on the butt for sure. I hadn't meant to yell so loudly. Answering the door and asking who it was first was new to me. I wanted to make sure I did a good job.

"It's Gram. It's me, Gram." It was my mother's mom. "Evie, you can open the door and let me in."

The person really did sound like Gram. Mother was home so I figured it was safe to open the door, and I did.

"Hey, Evie. Just the person I was hoping to see." Gram had a big smile. Gram was always in great spirits. I always wished we could have seen her more often. She came in.

"I love it when you visit, Gram!" I lunged in for a hug.

She laughed. "Okay, okay. Let me take off my shoes. Then we need to sit down at the table for a second. So I can show you something special. Okay?"

I was excited because she had something for me. I wondered what it could be. I tried to think of what it might be, but couldn't come up with anything. It wasn't my birthday.

Gram handed me a box with a lid.

It wasn't wrapped. It looked like a shoe box. This was definitely strange. I thought she'd brought me a toy, but why would she put it inside a shoe box? That didn't make sense.

A dish towel in her hands, my mother smiled at Gram.

I opened the lid and to my astonishment, it was a turtle. I couldn't believe it.

"I don't know how he did it, but he ended up getting all the way to my place! I noticed him one morning when I was out on the porch, sipping my tea."

I know my eyes must have grown bigger and bigger as Gram continued on, telling the story of the rescue.

"I said to myself, Gram? That looks a lot like Evie's turtle, Herman. So I put my tea down and I went over to have a look-see. By Jove, it *was* Herman! Isn't he amazing, Evie? I don't know how he did it, making it all the way to me. In one piece, none the else. What do you think about that?"

Her eyes sparkling, Gram waited for my reply, but I didn't say a word. I couldn't. I put my hands inside the box and gently scooped out the turtle. I carefully held him right in front of my nose. It looked like he was smiling at me. It was a turtle, yes. It looked sort of like Herman, yes. But I wasn't sure.

"He must have eaten well on his trip, Evie," said my mother. "I'd say he's grown at least an inch since we last saw him. What do you think?" My mother looked over at Gram again.

"Oh my, yes, he has grown. I wonder what he has been eating." Gram smiled at my mother.

My mother said, "Don't you recognize him, Evie? It's Herman."

Because my mother had said it was Herman, I convinced myself that it had to be him. Wasn't she always right about everything? She always told me she was.

"Herman. You're home!" That rare feeling of happiness spread over me. And I was relieved. Relieved that I no longer had to carry that other feeling anymore. That feeling of being guilty, once again, for something I hadn't done.

I would end up believing this story for over a decade until I wrote a school paper on it. A paper my mother read and was like, "Oh. He didn't really run away. I found him dead that morning. I don't know what happened."

Once again, I was the one who had done something wrong when I hadn't.

10

MY PARENTS FED ME TWICE a day. I ate breakfast and supper. I wouldn't even realize there was a thing called lunch until I started Grade 1. Back in my day, you stayed home in the morning, ate lunch—not me—then went to kindergarten in the afternoon.

I didn't have a lot of friends even when I was in kindergarten. No one wanted to spend much time with me. I'm not sure why. I wanted to have a best friend so bad. Other kids got invited to birthday parties and pajama parties. In kindergarten, more than half the class had birthday parties and invited kids from our class, but not me. It took me a while, but after hearing other girls talk about pajama parties over and over again, I wanted to know what they were. One day, I finally asked a girl in my class what a pajama party was. She laughed and explained it to me.

"It's when you bring your favorite pajamas with you and you spend the night at your best friend's house. It's so much fun. But you can't go to one because you don't have any friends!"

After she laughed in my face there was no way I was going to ask her what pajamas were. I always slept in my underwear. Panties. My favorite panties were the ones that had the days of the week printed on them. I felt extra special when I wore those. Whatever pajamas were, they seemed important. I could never have a pajama party over at my best friend's house if I didn't have a pair of pajamas. I wondered if pajamas would be easier to get hold of than a best friend. I spent a lot of time imagining what pajamas would look like, and what my best friend would be like. My best friend had to be a girl. Boys had cooties. It was okay to hang out and be friends with a boy, but not best friends. That was just the way things worked and for once that made sense to me.

I had two guy friends at school, though. I don't think they had cooties. I'm not sure why, but other girls didn't care to spend time with me. I wanted so much to be part of their group. I wanted to play house and be the mommy or be the teacher. I tried to be friends with them, but they would either ignore me, or laugh in my face. I finally just stopped trying. That was easier. I didn't get my feelings hurt.

Tony and I were good friends for a while, playing together during recess. Then one day, he just stopped coming to school. I'm not sure what happened, I just never saw him again. The other guy, Paul, had no other friends, either. No one wanted to play with him because he was different. I would rather be different than the same as everyone else. I just didn't like it when other people didn't like me. It bothered me when I didn't know *why* they didn't like me.

The reason Paul was different was because he looked different. He didn't have two thumbs and eight fingers like everyone else in our class. He had two thumbs and *four* fingers. The rest were short little stubs of skin. I'm not sure if it was true or not, but I heard he got hold of an axe when he was three years old and had tried to chop some wood all by himself. He'd been alone, unsupervised, and had cut a good portion of his fingers off. He had lived on a farm at the time, but after the accident, his family sold the farm and moved. He had no other brothers or sisters and was always nice to me. None of the kids wanted to play with him, either. I figured if no one wanted to play with him, that was fine. We would start our own club. If you were at least two people, you could call it a club. That's what the other kids said. I found this out when I declared to everyone during recess once that I was in a club. They asked me who else was in the club with me. I told them it was just me and they laughed and explained how I needed at least one other person.

Paul and I would chat and hang out together during recess. He didn't talk much, but that was okay. I probably talked enough for both of us. At home, my constant chattering, trying to figure out what was normal, how to react, wondering what was going to happen next, was not appreciated. In fact, usually at least once a night, one of my parents would tell me to shut up. They never seemed to want me around ever. I wished they would play games with me, or read to me before I went to sleep. I heard some parents did that with their children every night.

I also heard that some mothers baked cookies and cakes with their children.

I heard a lot of things that would have made my life very different.

11

A T SCHOOL, AFTER WE CAME back from the weekend, kids would talk about spending time with their families, baking with Grandma, going apple picking, carving pumpkins, having family suppers for no special reason or occasion, watching movies…

I know my eyes would widen in amazement and I would feel a pain in my stomach, like a hunger pain, while I listened to these kids, with jealousy. I constantly wondered why my family wasn't like that. It made me hope my parents might change. Hope beat eternal for me, but in my stomach.

I remember once I got into an argument with my mother. I was about five and still in kindergarten. I'm not sure exactly what happened, but I was upset about something, and she didn't care. I remember that it wasn't cold outside and there wasn't any snow on the ground. It was probably early in the school year, September or October. I was upset with her, and she told me if I didn't like it, I should pack up my stuff and leave.

That had sounded like a great idea to me. I didn't have a plan or anything, but it still sounded good. It even sounded exciting. Like a new adventure or something. I wouldn't have to put up with my parents anymore. And since they didn't want me around in the first place, all of us would get what we wanted.

As soon as my mother said I could leave, I didn't need further encouragement. I walked right over to my dresser and got out two shirts, two pairs of pants, a sweater and two pairs of underwear.

I was good to go.

I folded everything up nicely. I couldn't find a bag to put my clothes in because my mother wouldn't let me take my school bag. It belonged to her, she said, but that was okay. The main thing was, I was leaving. I was running away from home. I was going to make it on my own.

This was huge. I couldn't wait until the kids at school found out about this the next day. Paul would be impressed for sure. Maybe the other girls would finally let me play with them. Then I worried that maybe they wouldn't let Paul play with us and I didn't want to hurt Paul's feelings. Maybe I would just stay with Paul.

I gathered up my clothes and held them close to make sure they wouldn't get dirty, or that I didn't drop anything. I didn't have a whole lot to work with, so I needed to be extra careful.

I went outside and I started walking. I walked right to the end of the block and then turned around walked back to the other end. I kept walking back and forth on the same block, over and over.

At first, I was actually *marching* back and forth, but eventually, I started getting tired. I wasn't allowed to go any farther than the block we lived on by myself, so since you can't run away without an adult, my options were limited.

I thought I had a decent plan going on. I hadn't really thought about where I was going to get food from or where I was going to sleep but I felt happy. No one was yelling at me. I didn't have any chores to do. I didn't have to feed my sister a bottle all the time. I felt independent walking up and down the same street, over and over.

Everything was going fine until, on the way home from his work, my father spotted me.

"What the hell are you doing?" He placed his hand on my left shoulder. His grip was tight. Even if I'd wanted to, there was no way I could move. I was paralyzed with fear.

This was not good. I had figured I would be long gone from the wrath of my father by the time he got home. I would be miles and miles from home by the time he came back. Then he would ask my mother where I was, and she would break down crying, telling him how sorry she was that she had made me leave and she would have to tell him that I was gone for good and it was all her fault. They would both be so upset, they wouldn't be able to continue on with their lives. At least temporarily. My sister, Dee Dee, would never learn to speak because her heart would be so broken by my absence.

"I'm running away from home," I informed him as politely as I could. I wanted to make sure we were clear that I wasn't pulling any stunts.

"Get the hell inside the house now before a neighbor sees you."

Dragging me by the arm, he started toward the house. I tried yanking myself free but he was having none of it.

"Mom said I could! She said if I wasn't happy, I should pack my clothes and leave. So I did!"

This wasn't fair. I hadn't disobeyed my parents. I hadn't done anything wrong. My mother told me to leave and now I was getting in trouble? I couldn't do anything right.

On the way to the house, I dropped some of my clothes. My father refused to let me pick them up, saying, "Too bad."

When I protested, he told me it was my own damn fault. I didn't have a lot of clothes to start with, so this was not good.

When we got inside, my father kicked my behind and told me to go to bed for the night. It wasn't even suppertime yet.

That night, I was not allowed to eat supper. I didn't get much sleep, either, because, of course, my stomach kept growling.

As if that wasn't enough, my parents got into a fight because my mother had told me I could run away if I wanted.

According to my father, this was also her fault.

I couldn't sleep also, because I kept hearing my father telling my mother she was useless.

I wasn't sure what that meant, but I figured it wasn't anything nice because I heard her crying.

I decided that the next time I ran away, I would not do it on the street in front of our house. Next time, I would do it in our backyard. My father wouldn't find me for sure. Then they would be sorry.

I still didn't understand why my parents were upset with me. It wasn't like they wanted me around anyway.

The next day at school, I stayed quiet and listened to all the other kids talk about their families.

The other kids loved their siblings and parents and talked about yummy food. It made me sad. I kept wondering why I couldn't have what they had. I wondered how I could get a family like they had. There was no way every single one of my classmates could be lying.

Then there was Paul. His parents loved him even though he was missing a bunch of fingers. I had all my fingers and thumbs but it didn't seem to matter to my parents.

12

ONLY A FEW DAYS OF school were left before I would be heading into Grade 1! I was excited to now get to spend the entire day at school. Each day, I would be away from my parents for the whole day. There would still be the hated weekends, but at least I'd be free of them for five days a week.

I didn't care much for TV because it was usually on news or nature shows. My father controlled the remote.

Weekends also meant chore lists and trying to keep quiet around my cranky parents. It was hard walking on eggshells.

When we had professional development days at school, and ended up with a three-day weekend, that was even worse.

Paul and I had talked about trying to convince all the teachers in our school that students and teachers shouldn't get *any* holidays except at Christmas and summer. To Paul and me, that seemed reasonable. The rest of the holidays we didn't need.

Paul said it was a genius idea.

The first stop would be to get Mrs. Sadie on board. Once she agreed, then Paul and I would go from classroom to classroom explaining to all the students our plan, and the teachers would love us.

Paul and I thought long and hard over the course of an entire recess, and decided our plan was definitely doable.

If we played our cards right, we could get the approval from our teacher right after recess the same day. The next day, instead of staying with our class, Paul and I would use that time to go from classroom to classroom to get everyone on board. I figured the day after that, the school would have a party to congratulate Paul and me on our fine work. Maybe they would even change the school's name. They would name the school after us!

Paul was excited. He said my name could be on the school sign first. Our school would forever be called EVIE & PAUL ELEMENTARY SCHOOL.

It did sound catchy.

We were sure the principal would have a huge cake to honor Paul and me for all our hard work. My incident with the coloring pencils would be long forgotten.

Our plan seemed airtight to both of us. We couldn't wait to set our plan in motion.

After the bell rang, and as Paul and I got back in line to go inside, we decided we needed to look like partners. This was his idea, and I thought it was a great one so I agreed.

We held hands as we entered the classroom and marched straight up to Mrs. Sadie. We told her we needed to talk and it was an emergency. I knew from firsthand experience that anything important to adults was always called "an emergency." I had the lingo down pat.

We explained our plan to Mrs. Sadie in detail. Paul even pitched in a few words, which must have been hard for him as he hated talking to adults, in particular, to teachers.

After we'd laid out our plan, we waited for her to jump up from her desk and exclaim how smart we were.

"Evie and Paul, that's a stupid plan. Don't be ridiculous. All teachers need time away from children like you."

I stared at Mrs. Sadie. What did she mean by children like Paul and me?

She turned to Paul and spoke to him directly, as though I weren't even there. (I think that hurt the most.)

"You shouldn't let Evie rope you into these little fantasies of hers, Paul. It's going to get you into more trouble than she's worth. Keep that in mind. You hear?"

"Yes, Mrs. Sadie." Paul glanced at me quickly.

I wasn't surprised. There wasn't really anything else Paul could do. I didn't blame Paul one bit.

Then she let Paul go back to his desk. She was done with him, but not with me.

"Evie? There is to be no hand holding in or outside of class. This is a school, Evie. You are children. Hand holding is for adults only. I catch you doing it again and you will be sent straight down to the principal's office. I won't tell you again. Do I make myself clear?"

I just stared at her.

"Any questions?"

She was scaring me. She was too close to me. I would have said whatever she wanted me to, right then and there, so I could go back to my desk. I needed this to be over with. Humiliated yet again. And sad. Sad because now, Paul and I would no longer be friends. I didn't think I could get through the rest of the school days without him.

"Yes, Mrs. Sadie."

She motioned for me to go back to my desk.

I walked back slowly and sadly. Mrs. Sadie had made it sound like it was dirty that Paul and I had been holding hands. I didn't understand why. I had seen other kids holding hands during recess. Mostly girls, but still, they never got into trouble from the playground monitor. I didn't understand what the problem was. I also didn't think it was fair that other kids did it all the time and they didn't get in trouble for it. I do it once and, of course, the teacher is upset with *me* and threatening to send *me* to the principal's office.

At school the next day, I was not looking forward to hearing the recess bell. Now that Paul and I had gotten into trouble and the teacher had warned him about me, I would have no one to talk to or play with at recess. Everybody was going to stare at me and make fun of me.

The bell rang. As soon as I got outside, I sat near a tree. At least I could talk to the tree and make believe about living in a tree house or something. I had to find something to do to keep busy during recess.

"Can I sit with you, Evie?" Paul asked me. "Are you busy?"

I looked up to see him standing right in front of me with a smile on his face.

"You mean, you want to play with me anyway? Even though I got you in trouble with the teacher?" Maybe he was just teasing me.

"Of course. We're friends. Besides, our idea is great. Teachers are dumb."

With that, he sat beside me and we talked about what color we would paint our tree house when we got older.

I liked Paul even more then.

I couldn't believe he still wanted to be friends with me. I was extremely lucky to have a friend like Paul.

13

B ECAUSE SCHOOL WAS SHUTTING DOWN for the summer, my parents planned a fishing trip with my aunt, uncle and two cousins. I was excited. We were going to spend the day together. I would get to ride in a boat.

Plus, whenever we were with Aunt Jess and Uncle Matt, there was always lots of food. Not to mention, my parents never laid a hand on me or yelled in front of them. It was always good for me to be out in public when my parents were concerned.

Aunt Jess loved cooking and I loved eating her food. She made such yummy desserts. The best part was, there was always lots. If you were hungry and asked for seconds, you never got into trouble. Aunt Jess would just hand over the plate of food, no questions asked. The first time I ever felt wanted or loved was on that fishing trip.

"Can Evie come with us?" my cousin Zoey asked my mother. "We're going to climb the big rocks. It'll be fun. We'll watch her. Honest."

I'm not sure why Zoey seemed to be trying so hard to convince my mother to let me go.

"Is Delly going with you?" My mother asked.

I had to stop myself from rolling my eyes. I knew my mother didn't care who was going with me as long as someone was, to make sure I didn't "pull any stunts."

"Yes, she is. Can we go now? Can Evie come with us?"

"Be careful. And Evie? You make sure you mind Zoey and Delly. They are in charge of you."

Zoey was two years older than I. Delly was older than Zoey.

I clapped my hands with excitement. An adventure! I loved hanging out with Zoey. I dreamed of being cool like Zoey someday. Delly was okay, but most of the time, she just kept reminding us that she was older. As if we could ever forget.

We arrived at the rocks. I was careful to do everything Zoey and Delly told me to do.

I was having trouble climbing up a boulder so Delly offered to help. I was glad for that. I wanted to make sure I didn't mess things up. They had been nice enough to invite me.

"Are you ready, Evie? Now's your chance."

I was nervous. I didn't know what to do. I didn't want to back out and be labeled a chicken. I would never live it down. If I chickened out, they'd never invite me to do anything with them again. No matter what happened, there was no going back. I looked down. I was about six feet from the ground. It was scary.

"Don't look down, Evie," Zoey yelled from above, from the exact place I wanted to be. "It'll make things worse." Zoey was a good climber. If she could do it, I was determined to do it, too.

"Ready, Evie?" Delly asked.

"Not ready," I replied.

Unfortunately, all Delly heard was the word "ready" and that's when she gave me the boost.

My chin ended up colliding with the sharp edge of the rock.

I don't remember falling.

I heard someone screaming. Or maybe that was me?

I think I passed out for several minutes because both my parents, and Aunt Jess and Uncle Matt, were suddenly standing over me.

Zoey was crying and in between sobs, she kept asking if I was dead.

Delly kept repeating that it wasn't her fault.

I was in panic mode.

I tried to ask questions, but they wouldn't come out. I'm not sure if that was because I couldn't talk, or if it was because I was afraid to.

I was probably crying. I don't remember. I do remember that my chin was itchy.

Uncle Matt wasn't a big fan of blood. Everybody knew that about him. When hunting, he could shoot, then skin an animal, but when it came to human blood, it made him weak in the knees to see it. Uncle Matt mumbled something then turned away from me. He was the one who said I had to be taken to a hospital.

That's how I knew my chin was probably bleeding. That's why it was itchy. I wanted the itching to stop. I wanted it to go away on its own. I was hoping—and there's that word "hope" again—we could stay and continue the fishing trip, the visit, Aunt Jess's yummy meals, but it was decided, and not by me, that I needed to get checked out.

And that ended the fishing trip.

The end of the fishing trip was upsetting in itself, but even more upsetting was having to go to the hospital. I wanted to stay and have fun.

The *most* upsetting thing about the end of the fishing trip was that we hadn't had time to sit down and eat any of the yummy food Aunt Jess had made.

My chin changed from itchy to hurting because I had to hold a piece of cloth against it to stop the bleeding. Everyone seemed worried about me, even my parents. And my parents, it seemed, were not even mad at me for ruining the fishing trip. I was hoping it would stay that way. It would really suck if I had to, one, go to the emergency room, two, miss out on the fishing trip and, three, get into trouble with my parents all on the same day.

Because I was a child and bleeding all over the place, I didn't have to wait to be seen. The doctor looked at my chin for one second and said yes, I definitely needed stitches.

I had no idea what stitches were. I had always thought they had something to do with laughing. Like, "He had me in stitches." But somehow I knew I wasn't going to be facing that kind of stitches. I'd seen a few medical shows on TV. Anything that went on in a hospital was never good news.

"It's okay. It doesn't hurt that bad," I informed the doctor. "I don't need them." I made sure my parents heard me so I wouldn't get in trouble over the stitches.

The doctor laughed at me.

"I'll be right back with everything I need to get started. You just hop up onto the bed and lie down. It'll be over before you know it."

This was not good. I had to pee. Bad. Then there was the trouble I was going to get into with my parents. I was sure stitches were going to cost money we didn't have. I saw on TV that hospitals always charged a lot of money no matter what they had to do. This one time, a woman on TV had to sell her soul to pay for her daughter's treatment. That's why I told the doctor I would be fine without the stitches. The last thing I wanted was my parents fighting over the fishing trip plus the cost of my trip to the hospital.

"I just need to go to the bathroom first and then I can do it." I told anyone who might have been listening.

"Evie?" My mother's face was stern. Her hands were on the hospital bench. "You wait here like the doctor said. It'll be fine. It won't hurt. I promise."

Everyone thought I wanted to avoid getting the stitches. I mean, really, where was I going to run off to? I didn't even know where I was. And I didn't know what stitches were. I had to go to the bathroom.

That was all. But no one would let me. My parents weren't mad at me right now, but if I peed my pants—made them look bad—I would get into trouble for pulling one of my stunts.

I gave up and lay flat on my back on the table. My mother was beside me, promising me she would let me have a chocolate popsicle after the doctors were done. They just had to fix me with a few stitches first.

Everyone else was telling me to stop squirming all over the place. Did they think I was in pain? Resisting? It wasn't that. It was because I was thirty seconds away from peeing my pants. My parents would be *so* mad if I wet my pants.

After they stitched me up, the doctor told me I could get up. I ran as fast as I could to the nearest bathroom while everyone kept calling after me, telling me I needed to be careful and not to fall.

I made it to the bathroom, barely on time, where I nearly cried with relief. I had not wet my pants. I had the stitches. Everything was going to be fine. My chin was sore, but it wasn't itchy. It was all bandaged up so I couldn't scratch at it anyway.

Surprisingly, my mother kept her promise about the popsicle. I left the hospital licking a grape one.

14

"EVIE! GO FILL YOUR SCHOOL bag with your clothes," my mother called out from one of the rooms in our apartment. "You can bring three toys." From another room she yelled, "The rest we'll get later."

She sounded like she was in a hurry. I had no idea what was going on but it had to be something important.

I always listened as much as I could to things that were going on around the house so I'd know what to expect, then how to behave. I couldn't risk being caught off guard.

An example would be when my father asked my mother if she'd had her coffee yet.

If she said "No," that meant not to bug her. At all. Even if I needed something. Even an emergency would have to wait.

Rule Three: Never bug your parents until they've had their first cup of coffee. (I think that would have been better as Rule One. I know it went along with keeping my mouth shut when we were out in public, and with Rule Two, don't pull any stunts, but I always got punished harder before they'd had their coffee, no matter what rule was involved.)

Listening: The key to survival.

"Why do I need to bring my clothes and toys?" I hadn't heard anything about whatever this was.

"I don't have time to answer all your questions, Evie! Please. Just grab your stuff. We need to leave soon."

"Where are we going?"

My father chimed in. "Can you just do what you're told for *once* and go pack your shit?"

I was scared from all the commotion going on so I convinced myself the family was going on an adventure.

It was nighttime. My parents hurried back and forth all over the place and they made a lot of phone calls. Most of them to people I didn't know, but some calls were made to family. Family members were asking a lot of questions, it sounded like.

Gram came by looking like she was about to cry. I wanted to hang out with Gram. but she was busy chatting with my mother and helping her pack things and assuring her that things were going to get better.

Next thing I remember, we were getting a drive to the bus station. I didn't know the man who drove us.

I could tell that my mother was sad, but my father was acting all excited.

I didn't think we were going to be on a very long adventure because I only had my school bag with a few clothes in it. My father had a large black garbage bag in one hand and my sister Dee Dee was holding his other hand. My mother was carrying a garbage bag plus my little sister Kelly, who was two months old.

I'd never been on a Voyageur bus. I saw them drive by sometimes, but I'd never been inside one. I didn't know anyone who had been on one, either. This was good for me. I couldn't wait to tell all the kids at school about my big adventure on a bus with its cool seats. They'd be impressed. I might even get a best friend out of the deal.

I loved the bus ride. But only for the first fifteen minutes. After that, I'd had enough. I had motion sickness and my parents hadn't thought to bring anything to give me to help with that. All the smoke in the air was bothering me, too. We were sitting in the smoking section. Dee Dee and Kelly kept fussing and wouldn't stay quiet.

One of the male passengers (he looked older than my father), told him to shut his kids up. My father got up and tried confront him but my mother got everyone settled down.

I swear that everyone in the smoking section was lighting up another cigarette as soon as they'd put out the last one. I couldn't stop coughing and my stomach felt awful. I didn't want to sit with my parents, but they told me I didn't have a choice. I thought if I could get away from the smoke, I'd feel better. My parents said I had to stay with them so they could keep an eye on me. I think they just wanted me to entertain my sisters.

The bus stopped once to let everyone off to go to the bathroom or grab a coffee or a quick bite. My parents found something at the shop to give me that would help with my stomach. I took it right away and after a while, I didn't feel like I was going to throw up anymore. I was glad. I hadn't enjoyed the bus for the first half of the trip because I didn't have time to look outside the windows or watch the other kids. I was too busy praying I wouldn't throw up. If I threw up, I'd be in trouble because that would be my fault.

At the time, I thought we were going out for the day. A whole day trip for the family would have been fun. No one had explained to me that we were moving. We were moving to Ottawa, an entirely new city. And we had no place to live until my parents both found jobs. We'd be staying with Aunt CeCe, Uncle Jim, and our cousin Jayla, who was around the same age as Kelly. CeCe was my mother's sister even though I didn't think they looked anything alike.

15

AUNT CECE LIVED IN A two-bedroom apartment. We were definitely crowded. Aunt CeCe and Uncle Jim shared a bedroom. My two sisters and I were put with Jayla in her room. My parents slept on the pull-out couch in the living room.

At first it was fun, like another adventure, but after a couple of weeks, all the adults were arguing and I was tired of looking after the other kids all the time. Two months went by before my parents finally found work, Mom as a cleaner for a big department store, and my father on a construction job.

We soon moved out, down the street and around the corner from Aunt CeCe's. This was great because we could still go visit each other. I liked chatting with Aunt CeCe because she always made the time. Not only that, but she was always working on some sort of craft and was always willing to answer all my questions or let me help, and even start my own projects. Aunt CeCe was always in a good mood and never complained or yelled. Uncle Jim was always drawing, and it was like magic. I could sit and watch him draw for hours. I could also ask Uncle Jim question after question and he never told me to stop bugging him, or to go away.

We had a corner store that was half the distance between our place and Aunt CeCe's. My parents and Aunt CeCe were friends with the family who owned the store, two Lebanese brothers. They were nice.

I loved going to the store. It made me feel grown up. Sometimes I wouldn't buy anything but would just go inside and look around. The brothers never seemed to mind. Once in a while they'd tell me I could take a chocolate chunk square for free. Those chocolate chunk squares had nuts and were my favorite. Sometimes my parents would send me to the store to get milk, bread or something else we needed, but didn't have the money to pay for it. When that happened, I would have to ask the brothers for store credit. I didn't like doing that. I was always nervous when I had to ask. It made me feel sick. It was even worse when I had to ask when there were other adults around. Half the time I went to the store, there would be guys hanging around, talking to the brothers. When I asked once what they were talking about, they laughed and told me they were just "shooting the breeze."

My parents never went to the store and asked for store credit so I didn't think it was fair that they would make me do it. One time, I went to the store and picked out bread, milk and a couple of other things. I got the to the counter with everything my father had told me to pick up and asked for store credit. The brother that was working looked inside a black book with lots of lined pages. That's where they kept a record of all the credits for the families.

"Sorry, Evie. Your parents owe too much money. They can't have any more store credit until they give me the money they owe me. I'm sorry. Tell them one of them has to come and see me to clean up a few things." The brother stared at me.

I was more scared than embarrassed There was a good chance he might have just signed my death warrant. I didn't have the heart to put everything back where it belonged. I just ran out of the store and back to my place.

I climbed up the stairs to our apartment as slowly as I could. I wanted to put off the inevitable for as long as possible. My parents were going to be upset for sure and it wasn't even my fault. I had done nothing wrong. I did what they asked me to do. I wasn't sure what we were going to do without those items.

My father spotted me as he was pouring coffee into his cup.

"Give me the milk. I need it for my coffee. I'll definitely need a few of these today." He smiled.

I didn't know what to say. It would have been easier if he'd not been making coffee. Was that his first cup of the day? I hoped not. If so, things would be even worse.

"Um. I don't have the stuff," I said quietly. I wasn't sure he heard me.

He stopped stirring the coffee and looked at me. "Did you not go to the store like I told you to?"

What was he thinking? Of course I'd gone to the store. Like I was told to do. I knew better than to disobey my parents.

"I did go to the store but they wouldn't give me store credit. I put the stuff on the counter like I always do and asked."

I thought he was going to slap me or something. I mean, this was my fault. Wasn't it?

"Okay. But did he say why he wouldn't give you the credit? There has to be a reason." He waited for my answer.

"He said he wants you or Mom to go to the store and speak to him. He wants you to pay what you owe him first. Until then, he said, there's no more store credit. That's what he said. Honest."

My father's right hand made a fist and he slammed it on the counter so hard it made his cup of coffee bounce off the counter onto the floor where it smashed into a hundred pieces.

I dared not move.

"All right. Go to your room. If I need you, I'll let you know."

Didn't he want me to clean up the mess he'd made? Maybe, but I did what he told me to do anyway. I went to my room where I left the door open a crack so I could listen. I was sure he'd want me to come back to the kitchen and clean up the mess. My mess?

Instead, my father went straight to my mother and confronted her. "Why do we owe the brothers money at the store? I gave you the money to pay it off when I got paid. What the hell did you do with the money?"

"I don't remember, but it must have been for something I needed. Nothing can be done about it now. There's no need to go all dramatic."

"I don't get paid for another five days. There's no milk for coffee or for the girls to drink."

Silence was sometimes worse than sound in our house.

"How can you just sit there? What we are going to do? The girls need milk."

My father slammed the apartment door as he left. I'm not sure how long he was gone, but we ate supper without him.

I was scared. I was wondering what would happen if my father never came back.

As I was getting ready for bed that night, I heard the apartment door open then close, then my parents talking.

"Where did you get the money for this stuff, Gabe?"

"Sold the bike. We will not be putting anything on credit at the store anymore. Do you understand? I mean it, Molly. This has to stop. I'm tired of this."

Silence.

"Now. I've bought myself a six pack. I don't want to hear any of your bellyaching. Give a man some space, will ya?"

I didn't hear a word from either of them for the rest of the night.

I often wondered what she did do with the money my father gave her. Did she spend it on those true crime magazines she liked to read? Or maybe on lottery tickets? Word search games? Crossword puzzles?

16

THE PLACE WE RENTED HAD only two bedrooms and to get to our apartment, we had to walk up several flights of stairs. At first it was fun having all those stairs, but when my parents did groceries, we had to drag all the bags up the stairs, down a short hallway and into the kitchen. We always had a gate up so my sisters wouldn't fall down. It was annoying having to constantly remove it and put it back.

My parents shared a bedroom and my sisters shared a room with me. It was crowded. Sometimes at night, my sister Kelly would try to climb into bed with me. I would feel her pulling at the covers. When that happened, I would get up and check her bed. She usually crawled into mine when she'd wet her own. I didn't want her to get into trouble. I always did my best to cover everything up and have her back in her own bed, asleep, before my parents woke up.

I remember celebrating my seventh birthday in that apartment. It was the best birthday because I was allowed to have friends over. I didn't invite anyone from school because I didn't have friends at school. I played with a few kids in the neighborhood, so invited them. I wore a purple and white dress with a unicorn on it and my cake was also purple and white. Somebody took a picture. I actually looked happy in it.

My parents' birthday parties involved beer and other alcohol, so my sisters and I always stayed in our bedroom, where it was safe.

My sister Kelly got drunk once. When she was two years old, so old enough to be walking around and getting into things.

My mother had been cleaning the house all day and had made herself a screwdriver (vodka and orange juice) and had put the still-full glass on top of the TV stand while she went to do something.

The TV stand wasn't high enough to be out of Kelly's reach, though. Had my mother not noticed how fast her daughters were growing?

Kelly recognized the orange juice and walked over to pick up the glass. She gulped it all down. The whole thing. She still had the glass in her hand, was licking and smacking her lips, when my mother came back into the living room to get the drink.

My mother thought this was funny but at least she kept a close eye on my sister for the rest of the day and even asked Aunt CeCe to come over and help with Kelly. Kelly was sick. Very sick.

I heard my mother telling my father that Kelly had the flu.

"It's just the flu, Gabe. Evie probably brought it home from school."

17

IN GRADE 1, WE STAYED at school all day. At lunch time, all the students ate at tables in the gym. No one went home for lunch. It took over two weeks of my sitting in the gym, wondering why we were wasting our time, before a lunch monitor finally noticed I wasn't eating like the rest of the kids were. I didn't realize we were supposed to be eating something called "lunch." Apparently, I was supposed to bring "a lunch" from home. I had no idea what a lunch was.

"Did you throw out your lunch again, Evie?" The old lady lunch monitor asked.

"What's lunch? I didn't throw anything out." I automatically became defensive. "I didn't do it. It wasn't me."

She was staring at me with raised eyebrows.

"Where is your food, Evie?"

"What food?" I lowered my eyes. The other students were looking at me. If I couldn't see them, maybe they couldn't see me.

Dolly, the younger female lunch monitor, came to my rescue.

"Cheese-on-a-cracker, Sherry. You're upsetting the girl right in front of everyone."

"I just want to know what she did with her food. I didn't see her eat it. Did you see her eat it?"

As my tears started falling, Dolly took my hand to lead me away from the lunch room and the curious stares of the other students. She took me down to the office. I had never been to the office before.

My heart sank. Going to the office was never a good thing. A principal would be there. I didn't want another problem with a principal.

Dolly told me to sit down. I was in for it now. I knew the principal was behind one of those doors. Maybe he was calling my parents right this minute. I was going to get a spanking for sure. I didn't even know what I'd done wrong!

"Your name's Evie, isn't it?"

"Yes."

"Does your mom or dad make you a lunch? Food for you to bring to school to eat?"

"I don't bring food to school. I never bring food to school." What she was saying didn't make sense. I ate before I came to school and I ate after school, when I got back home. It was silly to bring food to school. Why would I do that?

I kept glancing around, expecting one of my parents to come storming in to tell me to shut up.

Dolly sat beside me and smiled. She seemed nice.

"What is a lunch, anyway? Everybody keeps asking me about 'my lunch,' and I don't even know what one of those is. Am I going to get in trouble?" I was sure my tears would be in full-flood mode at any moment.

Dolly handed me a tissue. I blew my nose.

"Evie, when you're not in school… Like, when you're at home watching cartoons, maybe on the weekend, how many times do you sit at the table to eat?"

I smiled at her. I knew the answer to *this* question!

"Two."

"Two? Are you sure, Evie?"

"Yep. I have cereal or toast when I wake up, and we have a hot meal before I go to bed."

Dolly excused herself then came back with crayons and paper to color on while she "took care of things."

I spent enough time waiting for Dolly that I colored in two pages.

I went home after school that day expecting to be sent to my parents' bedroom where I would wait for my father to mete out my well-deserved punishment.

That evening, though, for some reason, my parents were acting nice to me. They didn't ask me what had happened at school.

Don't get me wrong, I was extremely grateful for this reprieve, but it was so out of character for my parents to be acting nice, I was even more guarded than usual. I walked on egg shells all night, waiting, but it never happened. Would it be merely a matter of time before this incident was brought up? Surprisingly, it never was.

The following day, as I was leaving for school, my mother handed me a plain brown bag. Inside was "a lunch." The "lunch" consisted of a peanut butter and jelly sandwich.

I wished she had given me a juice box and a snack as well, so the other kids would want to trade with me, but that never happened. And, of course, I never asked. Didn't dare.

***

Another surprise was this girl named Sally who came to my house every morning to walk me to school. She walked me home, too.

Apparently, a kid the age of six and a half was too young to be walking ten blocks, crossing, and turning through different busy city streets to get to school by herself.

I asked Sally why I needed someone to walk with me every day. I told her I didn't mind the company, that I even liked her, but that I preferred walking on my own. It made me feel grown up.

She told me it was her job to make sure that no one grabbed me and took me away from my parents.

I noticed she wasn't laughing when she said this. Did she know something I didn't? I wondered if that was why we left our other city. Did someone want to take me away?

The more I thought about it, the more I thought I might like to be taken away. Would my parents even notice? The new people might be nice. I would miss Dee Dee and Kelly, but it might be better for me.

I thought about asking my parents about what Sally had said. About being taken away, I mean. But I only *thought* about asking them. It wasn't something I would actually *do*. Not anymore. I was going to start keeping my mouth shut like my parents were always telling me to do.

See? Going to Grade 1 was making me smarter already.

18

A T THE NEW SCHOOL, I was having a hard time with reading. Each day, we were supposed to take a certain book home to read with our parents. We were to read it twice each night. This was so we could build our "vocabulary" and thus learn to read better and better.

I kept asking my parents, both my mother and my father at different times, over and over, to help me read and do my homework. By the end of the first week of school, I had been yelled at five times and smacked once. They "didn't have time for such crap."

Reading seemed important to the teacher and it seemed important to everyone else as well. What was I going to do?

Arithmetic was the same. Trying to make sense of a bunch of numbers didn't seem important. I did try, though, even though I hated it. We were supposed bring our math sheets—with the adding and subtracting—home to practice.

I didn't bother to ask my parents for help after the mess with reading, so I tried to do as much as I could on my own. It was both frustrating and frightening because I was scared I would get in trouble, either from the teacher or from my parents.

Back then, teachers used chalkboards. The teacher would ask questions and call on students to go up to the board, write out the problem, and solve it in front of the class. This was just as bad as reading out loud.

I always volunteered to clean off the chalkboard or the brushes, but was not picked once that year. You'd think of all the times it needed to be done, I might eventually have had a turn. But no.

I loved reading, but not out loud in front of the other kids. The worry made me mispronounce even the words I knew. I was afraid they'd laugh at me, even the teacher, even though they never did.

I would have to go through this ordeal maybe twice a week. It varied, which made it bad for me. If my teacher didn't call on me that day, I couldn't sleep worrying she might be calling on me the next day.

In Grade 2, a help teacher took me aside a couple of times a week. I loved going to see him. He was nice, and we played games so half the time, it didn't even seem like we were doing schoolwork at all.

He also came up with a cool way to motivate me. He knew I didn't like reading out loud but that was one of the things we had to work on. He would have a brand new book mailed to my house once a month.

My job was to bring the book in as soon as I got it. We would practice reading it back and forth.

When I knew the book off by heart and could read it cover to cover, with only three mistakes at the most, I got to keep the book! I got to bring the book home to keep it forever.

As soon as my help teacher started that particular reward system, my reading improved greatly. There was no stopping me.

19

BY GRADE 3, IT WAS one of my parents or Uncle Jim who walked me to and from school every day. After I was dropped off in the morning, whoever had walked me would tell me not to move a muscle or go off school grounds. No matter what happened, I was to stay on the playground until someone I knew showed up to walk me back home. This was one of the rules that actually made sense to me.

On this particular day, it was cold outside. It was after school. Leaves were falling but it hadn't snowed yet. I didn't have a watch, so I didn't know what time it was but all the other kids had already been picked up.

I was the only one left in the schoolyard so it was creepy. I was getting more and more scared by the minute. I was cold. I had to pee.

Once, I tried to get back into the school, but everything was locked. I didn't see a single teacher or anyone else I knew.

What would happen if I were still here when it got dark? The dark would come and I had no way of stopping it. And it was Friday. Not even the teachers would be coming back for days. What would I eat? Could I sleep under the play structure?

To make matters worse, it started raining. I didn't have an umbrella and I wasn't wearing a jacket. I decided not to go under the play structure. I wanted to make sure that whoever was picking me up could see me.

I inched toward the chain between the pillars, the boundary that separated the school from the sidewalk. Everyone, especially my father, had always said: "No matter what, never ever pass the chain."

All I had to do was get both feet over the chain and I would be off school property. I was definitely afraid of getting caught, but at the same time, it would be exciting.

I knew I couldn't stay here alone all night. I had to do something. The parking lot was empty. The playground was empty. The doors to the school were locked. Was this some sort of test? Maybe if I went past the chain link, someone from my family would jump out and tell on me and then I'd get punished?

I'd been waiting and waiting for someone to come get me. Had my family forgotten about me?

It was time to do something.

I'd been standing on my right foot, holding up my left leg to go over the chain for about thirty seconds, trying to muster last-minute courage, when I heard my name. It scared me.

"Evie! There you are!" My father lifted me up in a bear hug.

Huh? What was he talking about? Where else would I be? I was told not to move until someone came for me. That's exactly what I had done. Wasn't it? Or was I in trouble for looking like I was going to go off school property without an adult. I wasn't sure how to answer.

"Hey!" I exclaimed as cheerfully as I could. I decided ignorance was the way to go on this one.

My father put me back down, took my hand and we started walking toward home.

But my father never held my hand when we walked anywhere. He never talked to me either, except to remind me to pick up my feet when I walked, and giving me the odd slap on the back of my head for emphasis.

He seemed almost cheerful and I wasn't used to seeing him this way. He was a nicer like this. I wished he would stay like this all the time. Except that he smelled weird. Not like toothpaste or cigarettes, though. It was a familiar smell. I just couldn't think of what it was.

"I'm sorry, Evie. I know I'm really late picking you up but I lost track of time." My father looked down at me.

This was a change for sure, my father saying he was sorry. As far as I could remember, this was the first time he'd ever said sorry for something. He'd done and said a lot of mean things over the years and never ever said sorry. Today he hadn't hurt me, or said anything mean, he was just late, and he was saying sorry.

Something was off.

Yes. He'd been late. But I wouldn't have complained about something like that. I had learned to never complain. All it got me was in trouble.

"I don't want to go home right away to see your mother. I can't handle being around her right now. You know how she can be. How about I take you to McDonald's for a Happy Meal first? Just us?"

My parents were almost the same, both screaming, swearing and throwing things at each other. My mother never hit me though, it was always my father. Our glass ashtray collection was getting smaller and smaller as the weeks and months and years went by.

"Yippee!" I wasn't sure where this was going, but it was looking good. I wasn't in trouble and we were going to eat my favorite food.

I sat there munching on my Happy Meal. I was almost done so was already eyeing the fries. The fries were yummy so I always saved them for last.

"Your mother's going to kill me," my father said.

I stopped chewing and glanced around. Was my father talking to me?

"My boss and I got into it today and things got out of hand. I got fired, but I mean it wasn't my fault. My boss is a complete moron. I decided to blow off steam so I went to the bar. To have a few drinks, y'know? I lost track of time. That's why I'm late picking you up."

That's what the smell was. My father had been drinking.

I didn't know what to say. I didn't want to upset him. At the same time, I wanted to eat my fries.

My mother didn't find out he'd been fired for over a week. He got up every morning as if for work. He had her pack his lunch and everything like nothing had happened. Every time I would pass by him, he would bring his finger up to his lips to remind me not to say a word. He left every morning and every morning she would wish him a good day at work. He'd be out of the house all day and return like he'd just finished a hard day's work. He was doing a great job of covering up his mess.

That is, until the following Friday when it was payday and my mother asked him for his pay so she could go to the bank. (She looked after the banking stuff.)

My father didn't answer and didn't hand over a check. Because he was owed money for a few days' work, his boss had paid him, but in cash. And my father had spent it. He tended not to think very far ahead and hadn't this time. The jig was up. He had to confess.

My mother was furious. She started picking up whatever she could get her hands on and throwing it at him.

That was my cue to go hide in my room. I would still be able to hear the majority of what they were saying—be on guard if things got extra bad, like they sometimes did. My sisters came with me. We would always color until things quieted down.

I mentioned ashtrays. We used to always have two big, green ones, Those were the first to get chipped or broken during a fight and were soon replaced by new ones. As I got older, though, we had only the small, clear glass ones. I guess they were cheaper. And they did a lot less damage when hitting the wall or a person.

That night, my mother put a few holes in the wall and managed to get my father's left arm and his forehead, too.

One projectile left a permanent scar on his forehead, and every time I looked at my father after that, it brought back reminders of that night. Reminders of all the yelling, swearing, punching holes in the walls, objects flying, all while my sisters and I were trying to pretend it wasn't happening.

This wasn't the first time I took charge of my sisters when things got bad, and it wouldn't be the last. My sisters were getting used to what I started thinking of as The Drill, so they always did what I told them to, without question. I felt bad for them. They shouldn't have had to deal with anything like that. They were kids. But wait. I was a kid, too. I was eight years old when that one happened.

20

AT THIS SAME SCHOOL, I ended up scoring another set of stitches. This time, it happened on Halloween day. Back then, the kids dressed up and we played games. We had fun.

I was a witch, with green make-up and a big black witch hat. I even had two cookies for lunch. Usually, I just got the same old peanut butter and jelly sandwich so I couldn't wait to eat the cookies. Of course, the morning dragged on and on forever. It always does when you're looking forward to something.

I was actually tempted to eat my cookies before I ate my sandwich, but somehow thought my parents might find out. Maybe it would show on my face, or my teacher or someone else would tell on me. I could never be too careful with a delicate situation such as this. I was having a good day and there was no point in spoiling it on something like this. It just wasn't worth it.

I ate my sandwich quickly. I took out the first cookie and snapped it in half to make it last longer. In my reasoning, I now had three cookies.

I took a bite of the yummy chocolate chip cookie. It tasted so good, I actually closed my eyes. Chocolate chip cookies were my absolute favorite.

Maybe I would get cookies in my lunch now all the time? That would be awesome. If I had cookies, maybe someone would actually want to trade with me. Not today! Today I wanted these cookies all to myself.

Suddenly there was a tap on my shoulder. I quickly opened my eyes. It was Miles. He wasn't popular, either, but in his case, it was because he was mean to everyone. He was always making fun of other kids and threatening them and stealing from them. I even saw him pinch kids really hard when the teacher wasn't looking. No one wanted to be around him.

"Gimme the cookie," Miles demanded while holding out his hand.

"I'm not giving you the cookie but if you have something to trade me for it I will." I felt cool even suggesting such a thing.

Take a look at me bargaining my cookies.

I was sure this episode would help with my popularity, especially since it was with, of all people, Meany Miles. I would definitely get some extra popularity points there. What a memorable Halloween this was turning out to be! All of this awesome stuff and I still had trick-or-treating to look forward to later!

"I'm not trading you nothing. You are going to give me the cookie."

"Why should I?" I mean, really. Who did he think he was? There was no way he was getting my cookie. I was prepared to die first.

"Because I said so." Once again, he held out his hand for the cookie.

"Nope."

And I got up and walked away to another part of the schoolyard. I had decided that this was the best plan to remove temptation from the eyes and mind of Meany Miles.

For the rest of lunch period, Meany Miles did not talk to me or demand that I give him a cookie. The situation had been resolved.

Or so I had assumed.

After lunch, the teacher lined us up because we were going to assembly to watch a Halloween play on the safety of going out trick-or-treating. Most of he kids were groaning that it was a silly play and we shouldn't have to go watch it. I didn't mind, though.

We headed up the first fight of stairs that led to the gym.

I was on the third step from the top when I heard his voice: Meany Miles.

"Next time, do what I say." And he pushed me.

I fell all the way down the stairs, landing at the bottom, all sprawled out. My face hurt. *I* hurt. I bought my right hand up to my face and it came away with blood. I stared at my hand.

People were rushing around me but I didn't move.

I think I passed out because I don't remember anything after that until I was at the hospital. I had split my top lip open and needed stitches. That was all. I would be all healed up within a few days. I was lucky, they said. Very lucky.

But they called my mother at work. She had to come to the hospital to be with me. She wasn't happy about missing work time. Pay. I couldn't believe that my mother gave me trouble for being clumsy.

I tried to explain what had happened. That I wasn't being clumsy. That I hadn't just thrown myself down the stairs on purpose.

"Really, Evie?" said my mother, her hands on her hips. "You expect me to believe that some kid attacked you and made you fall down the stairs because you wouldn't give him a cookie?" I never liked it when her eyes locked with mine like that.

"Yes," I insisted. "It was Meany Miles!"

"Child, you have such an imagination. You'd better be careful because someday it's going to get you into a whole heap of trouble." My mother walked away, shaking her head.

I tried explaining it to her again, later on, thinking she hadn't heard me the first time.

She would have none of it. Case closed.

Not only did my mother not believe me, but neither did my teacher. I tried to explain to my teacher that everyone was afraid of Meany

Miles. I told the teacher there were kids who *saw* him push me, that she should ask *them*. For one—well, I guess for two—the twins, Tim and Tom, had seen him push me. They'd been right beside me. There might be others.

You know what the teacher said to me?

"Oh, Evie. Your mother's right. You do have quite the imagination."

There were no more cookies in my lunch after that. It was back to peanut butter and jelly, jelly and peanut butter, peanut butter and jelly…

21

IT WAS EARLY IN THE spring and I was part way through Grade 3 when I had to switch schools again. We moved. Grade 3 and my third school. No wonder I had a hard time making new friends.

The new school was closer to our new place, so I was allowed to walk on my own, which was good. I didn't like having someone walking me.

I didn't like that I couldn't stay at school for lunch, though. Only kids who took the bus to school were allowed to stay. There wasn't enough room in the gym. Instead, at lunch time, I had to go to a sitter's house and have lunch with five other kids and then walk back to school.

What I wouldn't have given to stay at school for lunch! At lunch, you found out all the cool stuff that was going on. You found out what teachers you should be afraid of for the next grade, or why yet another supply teacher had gotten suspended. I was missing out on the crucial guidelines of how to survive elementary school.

My parents didn't get it. Sometimes I thought they wanted me fail on purpose.

My sitter was good to us but she had three kids of her own. That usually meant there were at least six kids running around all the time. I didn't like her husband. He was mean and there was usually yelling going on when he was home, which, I'm happy to report, wasn't often.

The first day we went to the sitter's, her oldest boy, two years older than I was, kept trying to kiss me on the lips when no one was looking.

He followed me everywhere.

I told the sitter, his mother, and she told me to tell him to stop.

I'd already tried that, I explained to her, and it hadn't worked.

I did what she said. I told him repeatedly to stop, but it still wasn't working.

On the second day, when he tried again, I warned him that if he tried to kiss me one more time, I would punch him in the face.

The sitter heard me and laughed.

He left me alone for a while, but eventually, he tried again. I curled my right hand into a fist and punched him. To my surprise, I managed to actually hit him where I was aiming, his face. I gave him a bloody nose.

I waited for the sitter to grab my arm and give me a few swats on the butt, but she didn't. She had seen the whole thing and was smiling.

I wondered why she would be happy that I would l hit her son. That was weird, wasn't it? His nose was bleeding all over the place and he ended up with a bruise that he had to explain to everyone.

The only thing his mother said was that maybe next time he should leave a girl alone when asked.

After that incident, that kid and I got along just fine. We still had our moments, but he learned to back off when he got annoying and I threatened to give him another bloody nose.

We usually had peanut butter and jelly sandwiches—yes, peanut butter and jelly at the sitter's, too—grilled cheese, or Kraft Dinner for lunch. For some reason, he and I called it Karate Dinner and thought that was the most hilarious thing in the world.

One day, my sitter asked me to go into her bedroom to grab something from her bed. I was happy to go. I'd never seen her bedroom before. The door was always closed. Was there secret stuff in there she didn't want anyone to see or know about?

I opened the door and went in to pick up the item from her bed. I took a moment to spin around and look at everything quickly.

My eyes stopped half way and locked onto the shelves on the wall across from her bed.

There were three wide shelves filled with what looked like fuzzy slippers. This was cool. Where had all the slippers come from?

As I handed the sitter the item she'd asked me to get, the thought occurred to me that maybe she worked for Santa. Santa had plenty of people all over the world who helped him out. Why else would she have dozen and dozens of slippers? Who needed that many?

I asked her about them, expecting Santa's name to come up but it didn't.

She explained. Every Christmas, she and her family got together to give thanks, to see each other and to exchange presents. It was very expensive buying gifts for all her brothers, sisters, in-laws, and nephews and nieces, so she made each person a pair of slippers. She even let me watch her knit. Over time, she taught me how.

I learned three things from the sitter: how to knit a slipper, how to stand up for myself, and that peanut butter and jelly sandwiches are not so bad after all, it depends on the company you're eating them with.

22

THIS NEW SCHOOL WAS OKAY. "Okay" meaning not great but not bad. At least the kids would talk to me.

About a month before school was let out for summer vacation, we were in the schoolyard talking about our summer plans. I was with two guy friends. A few minutes earlier, I'd been playing jump rope with a couple of girls and I was happier than a bug in a rug until I got kicked out of the game because I wasn't any good at it. A bunch of the older kids, grade six, mostly boys and one girl, decided they were going to have a race to see who the fastest runner in the entire school was. Whoever won the race would be the fastest runner in the entire school! They would have bragging rights for a long time!

So there I was, minding my own business, chatting with friends. Like, one minute I'm laughing about something that was said: one of the guys had a dog named Poo! It was short for Winnie-the-Pooh. The next minute, I'm lying flat on the ground kissing the pavement and in pain.

At first, I didn't move because I was trying to figure out what had happened. The kid who had the dog named Poo told me I'd better get up or I'd get trampled again.

As recommended, I got up but the Poo owner pointed at my face, yelled out that it was bleeding, that it was gross, then took off. Great friend, wasn't he?

I had no idea who had trampled me and no one stepped up to admit it.

The bell rang.

Recess was over.

I got in line.

One of the lunch monitors yelled at a the two kids standing near me, both to the side of me, one ahead and one behind. They were told to get into line, straight, like they were supposed to.

"But her face is bleeding. It's gross. She should clean herself up."

With wide eyes, the lunch monitor walked over to me. "Your name's Evie, isn't it?"

"Yes." Was I in trouble because I'd wrecked the race?

"Come with me. Everything's going to be fine. Just fine. No worries." She put her arm around me and guided me toward the principal's office, all the while mumbling the word "fine" over and over again. I wondered if there might be something wrong with her.

At the office, the secretary immediately came over with paper towels. Someone else went to call my parents.

Yes. I ended up back in the hospital.

Yes. My chin had been split open.

And yes, I needed stitches. Again.

After this incident, I didn't find a best friend, but the kids paid more attention to me for a while because they thought it was awesome that I had to wear a bandage on my face to cover up the stitches.

The doctor removed the bandage a few days later, saying the stitches would fall out on their own. I wasn't sure what that meant, but the kids at school kept hanging around me hoping to actually witness the stitches falling out. One kid kept telling everyone that once all of my stitches had fallen out, my face would split open again. That had me worried. The last thing I wanted was another set of stitches.

Two weeks after the incident, the kids were no longer interested in my chin or my stitches or in me. My claim to fame had been short-lived and things went back to the way they used to be.

None of the kids involved in the race got into any trouble. Typical. Somehow my imagination, my "quite the imagination there, Evie," had once again made it my fault. Amazing.

23

THEN THERE WAS THAT TIME my mother went to bingo with her friends. She often went to bingo, and usually when she went out with her friends, my father went out with his and they would get us a babysitter.

Our babysitter for that kind of evening would be a teenage girl from the neighborhood. There were different ones. I had one favorite: Trina.

My mother had left for bingo and I was waiting for the babysitter to show up. My father would leave and things would be quiet. By the time my parents got home, I would be sleeping. A quiet evening with no fighting or flying objects. I was very much looking forward to it.

"That bites," I heard my father say as he hung up the phone.

I didn't say a word. If he wanted me to know what was going on, he would tell me. There was no point in getting myself into trouble for asking about something. Asking questions got me labeled as a Nosy Parker.

"I guess you're stuck with me tonight. I'm not going out? No need for a sitter. What are you looking so worried about? We'll be fine. I can handle this."

Generally, my father was never left with us for very long. Tonight, we would be alone for two or three hours. I should go to bed early, I thought, to save us some awkward moments. I doubted if I could sit in the living room watching nature shows all evening with my father. Or, the worst, sit still while he watched the news.

Quietly, I sat down on one of the chairs. I wasn't expecting my father to entertain me the entire time, but I figured he might at least chat for a few minutes. Since I didn't want it to look like I was avoiding him, I decided not go to my bedroom right away.

For now, he just seemed to be thirsty. He'd already consumed about four beer.

"Hey! I got an idea." My father slapped his hand on his knee.

I waited in silence to hear this amazing idea of his. Amazing? No. My father's ideas were never amazing. They usually ended up in a fight with my mother, or costing money which still ended up in an argument. Either way, I knew things were not going to turn out well.

"Just because the guys bailed on me, that doesn't mean I can't still get a few runs in."

My father began to clean off the coffee table.

What was he talking about? And why was he cleaning off the table?

I actually wondered if we were going to start running around in our tiny apartment. It definitely didn't feel like a good idea in general, let alone something I would enjoy.

One of the things my parents fought over was that he *never* thought things through before doing them. They argued about my mother's spending, my father's friends… Not that my mother didn't like my father's friends, she did. It was because they had more money than my father did and he was always trying to show off, which never turned out well, of course. But the main thing was that he didn't think things through.

I held my breath.

"Evie. Go get those old phone books from your room. Put them on the coffee table."

I kept old phone books in my room to stack them for fun or to use them as desks when I played sessions of school with my imaginary friends. The phone books were also fun to sit on when they were stacked. Sometimes I used them as weights, pretending I was going for the Strongest Kid Alive medal.

I went back and forth from my room to the living room placing the old phone books on the table like I'd been told to do. It took three trips. I wanted to make sure I didn't drop or wreck any of them. They were my phone books and I needed them back after my father was done with them, so I could keep playing school. It had taken me a while to collect them.

***

After I'd stacked the phone books, I sat on the couch and waited. My father disappeared to my parents' bedroom to grab "supplies" as he called them. I still didn't have a clue what he was up to. I probably wouldn't have stuck around if I'd had one. I had no idea where I would have gone, but I'm sure I would have at least tried leaving the apartment.

My father returned to the living room, carrying his crossbow.

I had seen him holding the bow before when we were visiting Aunt Jess and Uncle Matt and they were getting ready to leave for the hunt camp. A crossbow out in the country would seem okay. Not sure what use it was in the middle of the city. There didn't seem to be much to hunt around the apartment.

My eyes scanned the room. My sisters were sleeping. There was no way we could just leave them here and go off hunting. That would be ridiculous. My father wasn't making any sense. I'd lost count of how many times my father had been irresponsible, but surely he wasn't going to leave the girls behind.

Or maybe he was going to leave me home alone with them and I would be the babysitter. I wasn't very comfortable with that idea. I was way too young. Even I knew that. I knew that my sisters were sleeping but what if they got sick in the middle of the night or they got hurt or something, I was too young to be left in charge.

My father looked at me, smiled, and let out a small laugh.

"What? No worries, Evie. Everything's fine. We're just going to do a little target practice. Hunting season's coming up. I got to be on my game. I can't just keep sittin' around waitin' for the right time to come to me, can I? I was supposed to go out tonight but look what happened. A change in plans. So. I'm going to make that work to my advantage. Always remember, Evie. If you practice, practice, practice, you get better, better, better. And no one can ever be too good at hunting."

I kept waiting for him to laugh or tell me he was just kidding but he didn't. He continued on like what he was doing and saying was completely normal. I had seen it plenty of times before. He was definitely drunk.

I was scared. I sat there waiting as he organized his stuff. I wanted no part of what was about to take place, but I also knew, deep down, that I wouldn't have a choice.

"I think I might go to bed early," I said.

Going to bed seemed like a much safer option. I gave myself a pat on the back for remembering my earlier idea.

But he stopped me from leaving the room and reminded me that it was a Friday night, that I didn't have school the next day. "Right?" There was no reason for me to be going to bed early.

"Just stay here and keep me company, Evie."

My father was in charge, the responsible adult, and I had to do whatever he said. The last thing I wanted to do was to make my father angry when he was this drunk.

"Get ready. No worries. Simple. All I need you to do is take two of the phone books and hold them together like this."

He demonstrated by placing one book on top of the other, tilting them up straight, then holding them like that.

I had no idea where he was going with this but I grabbed two books and imitated him. So far so good. This didn't seem too difficult.

"Good, good. Just like that. Now bring them with you and stand at the door. Yep. Just like that. Right there. Stand right in front of the apartment door."

My father was referring to the main door of the apartment leading to the outside world. All the doors in our apartment were awesome. We had thick, puffy vinyl doors. Each door was a different color with metal bolts designed into a shape. The back of our front door to the apartment was green vinyl in the shape of a large diamond. When we moved into this apartment, all the doors were already like this. Everyone thought it was cool and so did I.

I walked over to the front door and stood with the books. My father came over and did something on the door.

"Just making sure it's locked." He sounded like he knew what he was doing. I had my doubts. "We don't want to have any accidents. You know. In case someone barges in with you standing right there? That would *not* be a good thing. At all."

The night was getting stranger by the minute. Who would dare barge through our front door knowing that my father lived there? Ah. My mother would. I began to hope she might come home early, walk through that door, put a stop to whatever nonsense was taking place.

A small part of me felt relieved. My father was thinking of my safety. He didn't want me standing at the doorway and possibly getting banged if somebody came in.

I held the two phone books in front of me and to the right as instructed.

My father inserted an arrow into his crossbow.

"Evie. Stop shaking. You're moving the target around." He was getting impatient which made me even more frightened. I now understood what he was planning to do.

He pointed the crossbow downward to pull back the wire and hook the arrow in.

He stood straight and readied his stance. "Stop shaking."

Fine for him to say. He wasn't the one with a deadly weapon pointing at him.

The creepy part was the expression on his face. He was smiling.

I couldn't stop shaking. I was so scared, I thought I might pee my pants. That was something I could *not* do, no matter what. How could this be happening? Maybe it was a dream. Maybe I did have "quite the imagination, Evie." I closed my eyes and counted to ten. Slowly. With any luck, I'd wake up in my bed. Wake up from this dream. Dream? Nightmare.

I made it to nine before I was suddenly slammed against the door frame from the impact of the arrow hitting the phone book, the target. I couldn't hold it in any longer. My father had literally scared the pee right out of me. Urine dribbled down my pant legs, making a large wet spot. I was paralyzed with fear. All I could do was pray my father wouldn't notice.

Maybe it was over. Surely my father had come to his senses. But of course I was wrong.

"Evie! Did you see that? I nailed it!" My father was excited. He pumped his fist in the air and got ready to set up another arrow.

Please no. I bit down on my bottom lip and the metallic taste of blood told me I wasn't imagining this. It was real. I was in hell.

My father's second arrow missed the target—and me. It pierced the door and was lodged in tightly. My father walked over to inspect the arrow.

"Would you look at that." He pointed to the arrow as though I hadn't seen it on my own. I wasn't listening. I was hoping he wouldn't notice the wet spot on my pants.

"I missed. I missed. I fucking missed!" My father was no longer doing fist pumps. He had missed the target and was not happy about it.

Good. Maybe he'll stop this madness.

Nope.

He went to the kitchen, opened the fridge, grabbed another beer, popped it open and sucked back the entire bottle.

"That's just what I need. I won't miss next time." It almost sounded like he was talking to me.

Peeing myself was one thing. I might be able to cover that up, but if I did anything else in my pants, there'd be no hiding it. I would get a spanking for sure. I wondered how he was going to explain this to my mother when she got home. He'd gotten himself into situations before, but I think this one would be at the top of the list.

I watched my father load another arrow and take aim. I closed my eyes. This time, I heard a loud *thwack*, but didn't physically feel the impact as much because the arrow had missed the phone books and me again.

Yet another arrow was lodged in the vinyl door.

My father stayed where he was for a moment. He said nothing, just shook his head.

"Okay, Evie. Looks like we're done. I'm not so sure this is such a good idea." He went back to the main bedroom.

Was he going to pop back out in a minute and be ready to go again? Or maybe he had another idea not related to the crossbow. Maybe up next was an idea to do with his guns.

I waited for as long as I could but he didn't reappear. I took this as a good sign and decided it was safe to put the phone books back in my room.

I changed out of my wet pants into clean ones. I buried the wet ones at the very bottom of my laundry bag. By the time my mother and I did the next laundry, they'd be dry and no one would have to know about this terrifying experience.

I heard my father in the living room and I didn't want to leave him alone until my mother came home. After all, my two little sisters were still in the apartment. Once my mother came home, she could keep an eye on my father. He was her responsibility, not mine.

But until then, I had to keep my wits about me. He was trying to pull the arrows out of the door but he wasn't having any luck.

"Do you want help?" I asked. I didn't want to get into trouble and I didn't want my father in trouble because that would lead to arguing and perhaps more flying objects. I knew he was trying to get the arrows out so my mother wouldn't know what had happened. I guess he didn't want that whole What Were You Thinking speech again tonight. I didn't want to tell my father, that even if he pulled out the arrows, there was still a good chance that the holes in the door would be noticeable.

"I don't think so. They seem pretty stuck, Evie. This is not good. Your mother's going to be pissed off."

I stayed there with him in case he asked me to do something.

The arrows were still stuck in the door when my mother's voice on the other side of it called out, "Let me in! I forgot my keys. Yippee. It's mine!"

My father and I quickly glanced at each other. What was going on?

He unlocked the door and slowly opened it.

Hands waving in the air and talking a mile a minute, my mother rushed in, nearly bowling my father and me over.

"Molly. Calm down. You're talking too fast. I can't understand a damn thing!"

"I did it. I did it!" My mother was dancing around the living room.

This was something new. I'd never seen her like this before. Happy. Dancing.

I gave the situation maybe two more seconds before one of them would be getting upset and it turned in to a full blown argument, signaling my fast exit to my bedroom.

"I won. I won a thousand dollars at bingo!" She threw her arms around my father and kissed his cheek.

"Are you serious? You'd better be, eh? Money's not something to joke about. Never ever joke about money." My father was wagging his right pointer finger at her.

"I'm not joking. I got it right here." With that, my mother reached into her purse with her left hand and pulled out a wad of bills.

Dancing again, she started tossing them around the living room as she moved from spot to spot.

Laughing loudly now, my father threw his hands up in the air.

My parents were happy. Both of them were happy. Simultaneously happy.

As I stood there, not knowing what to do or say, I wished it could be like this all the time.

"Evie," said my mother, bending down to me. "This is for you." She handed me a twenty dollar bill.

I ran to my room with it before she could change her mind.

For the next two days, our house was peaceful.

24

ONE DAY, MY FATHER TOOK my sisters and me to a "target range." It wasn't an official one or anything. Several of his friends met us there.

Of course, no one else had brought their kids. My job was to sit on the rocks with my sisters and make sure they didn't go wandering too far. Boring.

There was nothing to do, and we couldn't move around because my father said it wasn't safe. All we did was sit on a pile of rocks about thirty feet from where the men were shooting at targets.

Every single time I heard a gunshot, no matter who'd fired it, I felt like I was going to wet my pants. My sisters were okay the first couple of times, but then they started crying. Who could blame them?

My sister Dee Dee kept telling me she was scared, and Kelly kept nodding her head in a *yes* motion every time Dee Dee opened her mouth.

I couldn't tell what the men were shooting at, but the targets weren't the paper ones with the circles and the dot in the middle that I'd seen on TV. The men were throwing things up in the air, shooting them, and they all seemed to be getting a kick out of it. Everyone was laughing, especially my father.

Later that night at home, my mother opened the cupboard to grab plates for supper.

"Gabe? There aren't any dishes in the cupboard. Did you move them?"

I thought I could help by walking around the kitchen and looking here and there. No plates. Anywhere.

"Don't have a clue what you're talkin' about, Molly." My father was in the living room, in his comfy chair, watching TV.

"Help me, Evie. They have to be somewhere. This is completely ridiculous."

We opened the cupboards. We still had coffee mugs and bowls, but not a single plate.

My mother started slamming cupboard doors. "What the hell? Gabe? They didn't just get up and walk away!"

No response came from my father. Case closed.

The plates were obviously gone. There was nothing else I could do to help so I headed back to the living room.

As I passed by my father he grabbed my arm, and not gently, either. "Don't you dare tell her we used them for target practice."

That night, supper was served in mugs and bowls and the following day, my mother bought another set of dishes and the incident was never brought up again.

Years later, I told my mother what had really happened to the plates.

"Seriously, Evie? The very thought of your father doing something like that is absolutely ridiculous."

My point exactly.

25

MY FAVORITE BABYSITTER WAS TRINA. She never yelled at me and was always nice to my sisters and me. When I did get in trouble, she took care of it and never mentioned it to my parents.

During the summer, she was the only sitter we had. She would pack a lunch, bring a blanket, a jug of juice, and we'd spend the entire day down at the pool. We'd be there as soon as the pool started filling up with water and we'd still be there when the pool was being drained.

I loved being with her. It was always fun. There was lots to do at the pool. We would swim, play at the park that was close by, and the pool always had art supplies, and things to make bracelets with.

I was in Grade 6 when it happened.

Trina had been out with her friends at a party. She was not the one driving, the car she was a passenger in was hit by a drunk driver.

The car she was in then collided with a guardrail and was cut in half. No one in her car survived.

I couldn't believe she was gone. She was nineteen.

I remember holding the article from the newspaper in my hand. I carried it around with me for weeks. I couldn't help but keep taking the article out and reading it over and over again. Like somehow that could change things.

***

My sisters went everywhere with me and I resented that. Dee Dee was the shy sister. Kelly was vocal and right to the point. I was both.

I remember one Easter. Beautiful weather. It was nice enough to jump rope. I don't remember exactly how old I was, but I wasn't in junior high yet, so I must have been about nine or maybe ten years old, my sisters, four and five.

For Easter that year, my sisters and I had been given chocolate and new skipping ropes. Whenever it was nice outside, my parents would tell us to go out and play. We'd be out there for hours, allowed in only when it was time to eat, but only sometimes when we had to go to the bathroom. More than once, we had to bug neighborhood kids to ask their parents if we could use their bathroom. I didn't like doing this, but didn't have much of a choice.

I had tied the skipping ropes together to make a longer one so we could play jump rope. We were all playing nice and taking turns.

It was going to be Dee Dee's turn, but for some reason, she didn't want to stand inside the long rope, she wanted to play jump rope.

I tried to explain to her that we had to take turns. Kelly and I had already had our turn inside the rope and now it was hers.

I don't know what got into Dee Dee that day, but she raised her right hand and slugged Kelly right across the face. I mean, she hit her hard. I was in shock and right away, of course, Kelly started crying. My father heard the commotion and looked out through our living room window.

"What the hell's going on out there? Evie? Shut her up. She'll wake up the whole goddamn neighborhood."

My thought was that my father was going to wake up the neighborhood with all his yelling, but I didn't dare say a word.

"Dee Dee slapped Kelly across the face. That's why she's crying."

"I did not," yelled Dee Dee. "Evie's the one who hit her!"

I couldn't believe it. It was like Dee Dee had been kidnapped and taken over by an alien.

"I did not. It was you."

Kelly chimed in. "It was Dee Dee."

My father disappeared from the window to march right up to where we were playing.

Between sobs, Kelly took her hand off her face so my father could see the bright red mark on her cheek. "Dee Dee hit me. She hit me hard."

Roughly, my father grabbed me by the arm then dragged me along with him back inside the building.

All the way up the stairs to our apartment, he kept kicking me with his construction boots. I screamed with each blow. It hurt. I'd had spankings before, but this was a whole new level of pain.

Once inside, he threw me onto my bed and slammed the door behind him as he left.

I was allowed to use the bathroom. I was not allowed supper that night.

The next day was Easter Monday and I was allowed out of my room, but I could barely move I was so sore. Bruises had formed. I didn't dare sit in the living room with the family to watch TV because every time I moved, I'd wince in pain, and either my mother or my father would tell me to smarten up.

At school on the Tuesday, I was still so much in pain, I had trouble walking. Gym class was a nightmare.

My teacher finally asked me what had happened.

I told her I'd fallen down the stairs. "I'm clumsy."

There was no way I was going to tell her what had really happened.

For one, she probably wouldn't believe me. But if she did, the school would contact my parents and then what? For two, I'd get into more trouble.

26

A COUPLE OF WEEKS AFTER THE jump rope incident, my father, out of the blue, told me to clean my room. I had my own room. My sisters shared.

He said I'd better clean it properly. I'd better not miss a thing. If I didn't make it spotless, he would throw out everything I owned except for my clothes. He would move me in with my sister Kelly. Dee Dee would get my room.

It was a Sunday.

I cleaned like my life depended on it. I even did my closet. It had taken me forever to get my own room. Obviously, the last thing I wanted was to have to share a room with either of my sisters ever again.

I came home from school on the Monday.

As threatened, my father had thrown everything I owned into garbage bags and into the dumpster. The dumpsters were emptied every Monday afternoon. Everything was gone for good.

I now had to share a room with Kelly, my younger sister, who, of course, went to bed earlier because she was much younger. That meant I had to sit out in the living room with my parents or go to bed early.

Over the next several months, my sisters would take every opportunity possible to tease me about how I didn't have any stuff because Daddy had thrown it out.

There was no way I would be able to have a pajama party with my best friend now (once I found one) because there would be nowhere for her to sleep.

I had missed a tiny piece of paper pinned under one of the legs of my bed.

***

Another time my father was left in charge instead of getting a baby-sitter, involved alcohol as well, but no weapons at least. I have no idea where my mother was. I was in my room.

"Evie. Get out here!" He always yelled. "We need to talk!"

I'd heard him loud and clear, but hoped maybe he'd just leave me alone. I was always leery when my father wanted me for anything. I'd learned from past experiences, hadn't I?

"Evie!" He was getting angry now. "Get out here! Now!"

I dropped everything and went to the living room. On eggshells as usual when he was around.

"Yes, Dad?" I hoped this wouldn't take long.

He smelled of alcohol. I had no idea how many beer he'd consumed by that point. I wasn't sure I wanted to know.

"Sit. Sit. Take a load off. You and I don't get time to talk nearly enough." He tipped up his beer and took a few swallows. "You're getting older now. There are things you need to know."

I sat on the chair beside him. This was interesting but I definitely didn't want to be any part of it.

"You know growing up there's peer pressure from so-called friends. You know, to do certain things. You need to know what to expect. So you're not caught off guard. Do you get me, Evie?"

What the heck was he talking about? I hoped he wasn't going to give me the birds and the bees speech. I was nowhere near ready for that one. Besides, it wasn't something a girl wanted to discuss with her father. Especially when he was drunk. I didn't know what to reply, I wanted whatever conversation we were about to have to be over and done with as soon as possible. The safest thing for me was to be in my room and away from my father.

"Yeah. I understand." I sounded much older and confident than I felt.

I waited to see what he would say next. Instead, he got up and went to the kitchen. He came back with a bottle of beer and a glass of something.

"Here. Drink this up." My father handed me the glass of pale liquid.

"What is this?"

I didn't want to drink whatever was in that glass. My parents never bought apple juice, which is what it looked like. The only juice they ever bought was the orange powdered mix called Tang. This was definitely not Tang, and just smelling the liquid made me want to puke.

"Well, Evie, as you know, alcohol and drugs can be addicting. Actually, you're pretty much screwed because both run in our family. There's lots of drug and alcohol addicts. Your grandfather was an alcoholic. I'm an alcoholic. You need to prepare yourself."

His eyes locked on mine. I hated it when he did that and it seemed, even though it sounded like he was warning me against something, he was proud that he drank. I was sure it was beer or some other alcoholic beverage in my glass.

The glass was huge and it was filled to the brim. I didn't even want to pick up the glass, let alone take a sip. What if I accidentally spilled it? But if I didn't try the liquid, he would be pissed off at me. If I did try it, and threw it back up, he would make fun of me.

I actually glared at my father.

"Take a sip." He pointed at the glass. "We don't have all night, y'know."

"Why do I need to drink this?" I couldn't believe I actually asked him a question and hadn't automatically just done what he said.

"Drink up, Evie. I already explained to you that addictions are a big part of our family. I am your father and I don't want this disease to affect you. The only way to fix that is to make sure you don't become an alcoholic. Drink it."

Did my father want me to drink a glass of beer to make sure I felt like crap so I'd stay away from alcohol and not become an addict? Yeah, that should work. Not.

I took a tiny sip of the gross-smelling liquid and tried hard not to spit it back out. It was beer and it was disgusting. I couldn't understand why people would drink this crap. It took willpower, but I managed to swallow a mouthful.

"There." I had done what he asked. He'd leave me alone now.

No such luck.

"You can't go to bed until you're done with the entire glass. Every last drop."

I figured the faster I drank it, the faster I could get this over with, but but there was no way I would be able to keep it down if I did that. I had to make sure I didn't vomit.

It took me almost an hour to finish the glass.

He actually kept his word and let me go back to my room.

I lay on my bed. Everything was spinning and I thought for sure I was going to puke all over the place. I decided right then and there that I would never drink beer again. Not even if ordered to by my father.

***

The next morning, my mother kept trying to wake me up for school, but as soon as I tried to move I would throw up. My head was pounding. I felt absolutely horrible.

"What's wrong with you?" My mother sounded annoyed. "Are you sick or something?"

"I'm going to be sick again." I cupped both hands over my mouth and ran to the bathroom.

One of the last times I'd felt anything similar to this was after the incident with my father's construction boots.

I thought I was dying. I kept vomiting. This wasn't normal. I should be rushed to the hospital. That wouldn't happen, though. My mother couldn't drive and my father was gone and there was no way my mother would call for an ambulance. If I called one for myself, they'd find out. It would be better if I died because I knew better than to tell on my father. Better to endure the pain than tell my mother the truth.

"Crap. I guess you can't go to school today, then. Your father's out. At work, I hope. I can't take a day off for this." She didn't seem all that worried about me. "Too late to get a sitter in." She picked up her purse. "Stay home. And mind yourself!"

She seemed upset with me. Not that I was sick, but as though I'd done this on purpose or something. I wanted to tell her what my father had made me do but I knew it wouldn't be a good idea. There was a good chance she wouldn't believe me. If she did believe me, they'd end up in a yelling match that I'd have to deal with.

My mother called the school and told them I had the flu.

My sisters had left for school, my mother had left for work and I was alone.

When I made my way to the kitchen to get a glass of water, I noticed a note on the kitchen table.

Out of curiosity, I picked it up to take a look.

What? She couldn't be serious. I double checked.

Yup. It was list of chores she expected me to have done before she got home from work.

She wanted the living room cleaned, dishes done and put away, and the garbage taken out.

I couldn't believe it. I mean, really. I'm puking my guts out and this is what she wants?

There were more times I stayed home because I wasn't feeling well, but not many, because every time I did, there was always a list of chores waiting for me. It was less painful just to go to school sick.

I ended up missing that day and the following day as well. I kept throwing up and couldn't eat anything. My mother wouldn't even let me take sips of water because she didn't want me having anything on my stomach to throw up. She didn't want to be cleaning up after me.

Instead, she gave me a wet facecloth to suck on.

My father told her I was faking. That I should be sent to school.

I guess he had taught me a lesson after all. If I DID end up an alcoholic, it wouldn't be from drinking beer.

27

G OING THROUGH PUBERTY WAS A nightmare. I know it's never a fun experience for anyone. I get that. But I was tiny and slow at developing, so waited and waited for my time of the month. That's all girls talked about around that age: getting their first bra and their first period. Without those two things, you were nothing. If you had one, you were at least acknowledged.

I actually prayed every night for either one to save me so I could be like everyone else. How was I going to find a best friend at this rate? And I heard one of the girls talking about her older sister's wedding. At a wedding, your best friend is what they call your maid of honor. No best friend meant I wouldn't have a maid of honor. Without a maid of honor, I couldn't get married. The pressure never ended. There was always one thing or another.

My parents finally started making me wear a training bra. Every so often at school, while I was trying to get my schoolwork done, one of the boys would grab the back of my bra and snap it.

Not only did it hurt, it was embarrassing. At least, I wasn't the only one being singled out. It was happening to a lot of the girls, but nothing was being done about it.

I never had the courage to tell on the boys, but I wouldn't have anyway because twice, I heard other girls tell and the teacher would tell the boys to stop, but they kept doing it over and over again as soon as the teacher's back was turned.

At home, my father started calling me Bra Strap, and now my sisters had taken to calling me that, too. It definitely wasn't fun being the oldest. I tried to get my father to stop calling me that but that made him laugh at me. My mother asked him to stop, but that made him do it more often.

I remember it well.

I'd been feeling off all day and the day before, too. I had a headache, and every so often, I'd get these pains in my abdomen. Nausea was part of it, too.

I told my mother but she brushed me off. I wanted to stay home but my parents refused. We were off to a barbecue at my parents' friends' house. I just hoped they didn't have any young kids they expected me to watch while the adults had fun. Usually, that's why my parents dragged me along. It was enough of a chore watching my sisters all the time, let alone other peoples' kids.

I was sitting outside in the friends' backyard. Not a single person was in the house. It was a nice day. We had just finished eating supper. There had been hamburgers, hot-dogs, chips, a bunch of different salads, and a variety of soft drinks. The food looked really good, but I could barely manage getting a hotdog down.

My sisters were kicking a ball back and forth across the lawn and were trying to get me to play with them. Thank heavens my parents were too busy having a good time to notice or else I would have gotten in trouble, not just for "neglecting" my sisters, but for being rude. Rude for not eating everything that had been served on my plate.

I was sitting at the picnic table as quietly and invisibly as I could, when all of sudden I felt like I'd wet my pants.

I was petrified. Not for how I felt, but because I was going to get into trouble for causing "A Scene." A Scene was worse than A Stunt. A Scene would make my parents look bad. Oh yes. Another important rule was: make sure my parents always look good in front of others.

My undies were wet. Gross. I was dizzy. I needed to get out of my underwear. I needed to take something for the pain in my abdomen. I wanted to go to bed. First, though, I needed to find a bathroom and figure out what was going on.

"What's that?" May pointed to where I had been sitting. There went my plan of trying to solve whatever was going on discreetly, and on my own. I turned to see what she was talking about.

To my absolute horror, there was blood on the bench where I'd been sitting. May came closer to look and then quietly ushered me into the house where she found my mother who was in the process of grabbing another drink.

"Um, Molly?" said May. "Evie has a small problem."

I couldn't wait to find out what my "problem" was this time. For some reason I hadn't put two and two together yet. Since May seemed to know what was wrong, I hoped she would tell me what to do so I would feel better. I just wanted the pain to go away and to make sure I wasn't noticed.

"What now, Evie?" My mother didn't even glance at me. Again, I seemed to be annoying her by my mere presence. "There's always something."

May looked at me. "Go ahead. Tell her."

May was out of her mind. I shook my head and said nothing.

"Molly, would you listen for a minute. Evie has her time of the month."

What? Seriously? The moment I'd been praying for and waiting for over the last six months was happening right now and all I felt was sick and humiliated? This was not how the wonderful scene had played out in my imagination.

My mother looked over. "Oh oh."

I wasn't sure if she was making a joke or didn't know how to respond. Or didn't want to deal with it. I suspected the latter.

"Mom? Can we please go home? I made a mess. Everyone saw. My clothes are ruined and I feel sick."

Surely this classified as an emergency. Would she, for once, take my side and consider my feelings? My situation?

"Oh, Evie. Honest to God. Don't be so dramatic. You'll be fine. This is nothing. Women have been going through this for centuries. You're not the first and you certainly won't be the last." She turned back to her drink.

May stood there for a moment and then gently placed a hand on my left shoulder. I guess she thought my mother would have stopped what she was doing to talk to me, or something. We waited a moment, with me staring at May and May staring at my mother.

"Come with me, Evie."

May brought me to her daughter Jazz's room. Jazz was a freshman in college so away at the time. May opened two or three drawers and searched through them.

Wasn't this an invasion of privacy or something? With May going through her daughter's things?

Hurry up, May. I need to use your bathroom.

I couldn't stay like this all night. I wasn't even able to sit down. How I was going to get home? There was no way my parents were going to let me in their car with me like this.

Then May pulled out a shirt, sweatpants and a pair of underwear and handed them to me.

"I'm sorry, Evie. There's not much else I can do. Go into Jazz's bathroom and get changed. The supplies you need are under the sink. If you look around, you'll find towels and face cloths. Help yourself to whatever you need to get yourself cleaned up. When you're done, just put them in the hamper. I think your clothes might be ruined so not sure what you want to do with those, but there's a garbage can in there, too. Take your time. I'll go grab an Advil and something to take it with. Things will be okay, just wait and see. I know it doesn't seem like it, but give it time. It's just a part of life for women. Seems like a curse now but it won't many years down the road if you decide you want children." She smiled at me, gently touched my arm, and left.

My own mother should have been giving me this speech. Not someone I barely knew. Again, I wondered why my parents didn't love me. If I had done something wrong.

I stayed in the bathroom for almost thirty minutes. I didn't want to see anyone ever again. Everyone was probably talking about me. Maybe even laughing.

But I had to go back outside to clean up my mess.

I changed into Jazz's clothes and got cleaned up. I felt better just doing that much.

May knocked on the bathroom door. I opened it. She held out a pill and a glass of water for me. I took both and swallowed the pill. I asked if she had stuff I could use to go clean the bench.

She smiled and told me not to worry, that she'd taken care of it. I didn't have to do anything.

Afterward, I curled up on the couch that was covered with garbage bags, just in case. I slept until my parents decided to go home.

During the next two nights, I was in pain. My mother made me sleep on the couch (with garbage bags) because my groaning was keeping them awake.

28

THEN THERE WAS THE OTHER time my father had a weapon. But this is a funny one and my mother was home at the time. Of course, he'd been drinking. My sisters were already in bed.

"I'm going to soak in the tub," she told him. "Going to have a nice warm bubble bath." She often sat in the tub for ages, reading a book. I couldn't wait until I got older and could read in a bubble bath, too. It sounded luxurious.

"Enjoy. I'm going to clean my guns. It's been a while. Evie? Clear the coffee table off. I need room. You can stay and help but only if you're quiet and don't start asking questions. The girls are asleep."

My parents always referred to my sisters as one unit, "the girls." Some people thought they were twins but they weren't. They were born less than a year apart.

I watched my father disappear into his room to gather his supplies. I think he kept everything under their bed. I just know I never saw it in plain sight. That was one of my mother's rules: make sure the girls (and she meant me in there, too, for this one) never have access to any weapons. That might just be the only rule my father ever followed.

It wasn't often my parents invited me to do something other than a chore with them. I was thrilled that my father wanted me to hang out with him. I cleared the table. I even fluffed the pillows on the couch.

Everything seemed good. I made him a cup of coffee and got

myself a glass of water. I set his cup and my glass on a side table so there was absolutely nothing on the coffee table.

"Don't touch anything." He placed the first gun on the coffee table along with some other gadgets and cloths then went back to the bedroom.

I waited for the action to start. It was nice and quiet. My parents were not arguing. They even seemed to be acknowledging the fact that I was there. That I existed. I wanted this feeling to continue for as long as possible.

My father came back with two more guns and a few other things he would need to take them apart, clean and reassemble them.

"Is that coffee for me?"

"If you don't want it, I can put it back," I said. Maybe he didn't want a coffee and I would get in trouble for wasting it. My parents always drank a lot of coffee and it seemed like I spent a good part of my days making fresh pots of coffee or cups of coffee and bringing it to them.

"Thanks. Good thinking." My father was smiling.

Wow. A compliment. Would an insult follow?

No. Not this time.

I sat on the couch, sipping my water, waiting to see if my father would need me to help, or if he was going to make small talk.

He took the first gun apart. He was quick. He was good at this. When he finished with the first gun, he picked up the second gun, worked on it but just before he began to take the third gun apart, there was knock at our door.

My father and I looked at each other. It wasn't often someone knocked on our door.

"Molly. Get the door. I'm in the middle of something."

"I'm still in the damn tub. Do it yourself."

I was never allowed to open the door, so that got *me* off the hook. But since I was right there, I thought he might let me answer it.

Whoever it was knocked again.

"Guess I better see who it is." The third gun still in his hand, he walked to the door and unlocked it. Remember I said that my father didn't often think things through?

He opened the door.

"Yeah? Can I help you?"

A guy in his mid-teens stood there staring at my father. Well, he was staring at the gun in my father's hand.

"Um. Uh. Sir. I… Uh. I'm here to collect for your paper. Sir." He took a step back. "If that's okay."

"Oh. It's time already? Just a sec. I'll go check with the wife. Be right back."

"No, sir. It's okay. Everything's fine." The paper boy took another step back.

"Wait. Wait there," my father insisted. "I'll check with her. Just a minute."

The paper boy turned and disappeared. I could hear his footsteps all the way down the stairs.

"What the hell's wrong with him?"

"Um. Dad? Maybe because you answered the door with that gun in your hand?"

"Shit." My father started laughing. It was strange to see him laugh. It didn't happen often.

We never saw the paper boy again. He never came to collect the money we owed for the paper we got every morning. We didn't pay and the paper just kept showing up every morning for almost an entire year before it stopped. After that, my parents didn't bother renewing their subscription.

29

I WOULD LISTEN TO THE KIDS at school or outside playing and chatting. They would talk about wonderful visits with their grandparents, what gifts they got for Christmas or birthdays, or their next vacation. A lot of the girls talked about dolls, their Barbies, hair stuff, dresses they really wanted, wished for. I thought most of it was silly because I had only one wish, to be able to shrink when I needed to. I wanted to be three inches high. That way, when I got in trouble, I could hide and no one would be able to find me. It would also make things easier for me. I could steal food from the kitchen, and the kids at school couldn't bully me if they couldn't see me. I wasn't sure how I could do it but was certain it would solve most of my problems.

Many of us have been bullied by someone. I know that because I was, plenty of times.

I got bullied because my parents were "poor." (They had money but they chose to spend it on bingo, cigarettes, alcohol, jewelry, clothes for themselves and eating at bars or restaurants.)

I got bullied for where we lived (in a project), because of how young my parents were, and because I had crooked teeth and had never been to a dentist. Dentists cost money.

I got bullied because I was never allowed to do anything.

I got bullied because I had to bring my sisters everywhere I went.

I got bullied for being skinny because my parents didn't feed me regularly, and bullied because my parents never finished high school.

***

The elementary school I went to only went to Grade 6. Then you "graduated" and went on to junior high. We would have a graduation ceremony and a celebration afterward.

One of the coolest things was our class was split into Grades 5 and 6. When grad time came, it was the grade fives who had to serve the graduating class. It was awesome.

I was excited about graduating. It was an important moment. I remember all the girls talking about their dresses and how they were going to do their hair and what not. This was news to me. I hadn't realized you were supposed to put some effort into how you looked for a grad. I tentatively approached the subject with my mother.

The best time to talk to my mother was when she was cooking. Never go to her room to chat or try talking to her while she was curled up on the couch. (I already told you about not talking to her before her morning coffee, even if you or one of your sisters had just severed a limb.)

"I need a dress for my grad. Nothing expensive or whatever but I need something to wear. Everybody's dressing up. Everybody'll make fun of me if I don't have anything. It can be an early birthday present if you want. Please. I need this."

"Kids make such a huge fuss over nothing. It's just a grad. Years from now, no one's going to remember a thing about it."

"It's not my fault. It's just the way it is. We have to get something."

"All right. We'll go this week. You'll have to find something on a budget."

My eyebrows rose on their own. The conversation over the grad dress had gone a lot better than I'd anticipated. Now that this part was over, I would have to wait to see if she actually took me to get the dress. Saying and doing was not the same thing in my family. My parents usually told me what I wanted to hear to keep me quiet.

I did get a new dress. I loved the dress. It was blue and white and looked like a sailor's dress. My father couldn't make it to my grad because he was in jail for something or other. My mother came, though. I was surprised but glad she was there. I felt good, and I was proud standing in my dress during this special moment.

Every year, three students from the graduating class were chosen as honor students. The students were chosen based on things like grades, leadership and a variety of other things. It was the moment we were waiting for. I thought for sure my friend Lacy was going to get honors. Everyone in the class had been talking for weeks about who was going to get the award.

Lacy and I were standing there and holding hands for luck as we waited for the principal to finish babbling and get to the important part, the awards.

"The three honor awards go to: Allan, Ricky and Evie."

The room erupted in applause.

I dropped Lacy's hand. I felt bad for her. We'd thought she was going to win. The kids that won were lucky. They'd have bragging rights for a long time.

"Hey. Evie. They're waiting for you." Lacy was pointing at the stage.

"For what?"

"They called your name. You won honors."

"Not me. You heard wrong." I shook my head.

The principal repeated the names once again.

"The three honor awards go to Allan, Ricky and Evie. Please come to the stage."

I couldn't move. I was scared. This was a mistake. Once I got up in front of everyone they'd realize it and it would be even worse.

Lacy nudged me, so I finally went up.

There'd been no mistake.

It was awesome. We got a special gold and white certificate, a medal, and everyone stood there clapping for us. It was like we were famous because our names were engraved on a plaque that was safely held in a show case in the hallway so all the teachers, parents, students and other visitors would see it every time they walked down the hall.

Even though I didn't have to, I asked to go to the bathroom twice the next day, just so I could walk down the hall and see my name on that plaque.

30

THINGS WEREN'T GOING WELL BECAUSE my father was home more often. The construction business in our city had slowed down so he didn't have a lot of work. We had just got a new car, and payments had to be made or it would be taken away. Things were getting tense so he called around in the Brockville area and learned there was work there, that he would be able to make some money, at least for the next few months.

He packed his bags and left to stay with Aunt Jess and Uncle Matt.

He worked during the week and sometimes came back home on the weekends. I didn't mind one bit when he missed a weekend. Things were a lot quieter when he was gone. They would argue on the phone sometimes, but that was a lot better than in person. A lot better. Things didn't get thrown around as much.

One night, later than usual, the phone rang, waking me up. I wanted to go back asleep, but I could hear my mother yelling from the living room.

"No. No. No. Liar!"

What's going on? Is someone in the house?

I heard a weird, loud wail. It was coming from my mother.

Something was wrong, very wrong. I ran into the living room to find her curled up in a ball on the living room floor, cradling the phone in her arms. She was sobbing so hard, her body was practically convulsing. Was this really my mother? This was strange. Foreign. I'd never seen her like this.

Carefully, and with as much gentleness as I could summon, I tried to take the phone from her.

She muttered something.

"What?" I said. "I don't understand."

"He's probably dead."

What was wrong with her? I had no idea what she was talking about.

"Who's dead? What are you talking about? Who was on the phone?"

I had managed to wrangle the phone away from her and I put it up to my ear.

Only the dial tone.

I tried to help her up off the floor but I wasn't strong enough and she was resisting.

"Your dad." She couldn't get anything else out because she was sobbing so hard. "Your dad."

At some point, Aunt CeCe showed up and helped me and my sisters pack. She was the one who explained what had happened.

My father had been at a bar. He'd had too much to drink. (No surprise there.) He decided to drive himself to Aunt Jess's and Uncle Matt's, drunk or not. Off he went in the family's new car. Off he went right over a small cliff, totaling the family's new car that he was in Brockville in the first place to pay off.

My father had survived, Aunt CeCe told me, but he was "in rough shape." They didn't think he was going to make it. "Your mom needs to get to Brockville immediately. She has decisions to make. She can't take you guys with her. She needs to be with your dad at the hospital."

We kids were to stay at Aunt CeCe's apartment for however long Mom was away. Aunt CeCe was sorry, but we would have to miss school.

That story was actually a pile of bull poop. Except for the drunk driver accident part, it wasn't true at all.

Yes, my father crashed his vehicle; however, he hadn't been injured. He'd walked away.

The investigating police officer's shift was almost over so he didn't want to have to fill out the paper work that went along with an arrest. Instead, he decided to just take my father to Aunt Jess's and Uncle Matt's, explaining to them what had happened.

Aunt Jess and Uncle Matt went back to sleep.

But my father was still out of it. He ripped a page from their phone book, grabbed the pen from beside the phone and scribbled what were intended to be his last words. His suicide note. He left the note on the kitchen table.

Uncle Matt kept his guns in the spare bedroom. My father grabbed one, opened the door that led onto the back porch, went outside, then pointed the gun at his chest and pulled the trigger.

It was poor Zoey who heard the bang and was the first to see my father lying in a pool of blood.

The investigating officers were polite at first, then ready to arrest Uncle Matt when they learned it was his gun. Then one of them discovered the suicide note. None of the family ever had a chance to read what my father had written because it was quickly scooped up and sealed away as evidence.

I don't know why he did it. I'm not sure *he* knew why he did it. I know most men shoot themselves in the head to commit suicide. I often wondered why he'd tried to shoot himself in the heart instead.

31

A UNT CECE LIVED IN AN apartment building. That day, both
elevators were out of working order. "Nothing new," she said.
"We'll just have to carry everything up." She lived on the eighth floor.

We'd reached the fourth floor when Aunt CeCe said a bad word
and pointed up. Yellow police tape crossed the stairway and there were
drops of reddish-brown stuff on the steps. "Blood," she whispered to
me as though this was nothing new either. She grabbed my sisters by
their shoulders and turned them around so they wouldn't see it.

"Down we go, ladies. No choice." We returned to the lobby and
walked up the other set of stairs.

The next day, Aunt CeCe's friend, Nadine, dropped in for tea, so
she claimed, but she was actually concerned about Aunt CeCe because
she hadn't heard from her in several days.

"Family matters," said Aunt CeCe. "Happens to the best of us, eh?
What happened on the stairs? We had to go all the way back down
then up again. The girls aren't used to that and they were already tired
from everything that's going on."

"You don't know?"

I quickly pretended I was engrossed in coloring my picture but I
kept the ear on that side of my head open. I was good at "multi-
tasking." I had to be, in my house. I had to always be aware in case I
had to take my sisters to my room, out of harm's way.

"Remember the weird couple on the sixth floor? Always arguing and dressed kind of strange, with all those bright colors and they both had purple hair? Well, it was them."

"Ooh, Nadine. Don't keep me in suspense. Tell me what happened."

"Well. You know the man. Always checking out other women. Spoken for or otherwise, doesn't matter to him. She found out he cheated on her. She confronted him. Huge row! He ran out with her behind him. She's saying she's going to chop it off." Nadine giggled. "Can you imagine?"

"Damn. Yes, I've seen her around. I wouldn't ever want to mess with that woman. There was blood so she must have hit him with something. No?"

"Yeah. With an axe. Why would anybody have an axe hanging around your apartment? But that's what she had and she used it."

"She got him. There?"

From the side of my eye, I could see that Nadine had crossed her hands across her chest and was smiling. "She got him and got him good. If you ask me, he got his just desserts. What you saw in the stairwell was nothing. The flight up is where it happened. I heard it from some of the other tenants. They were there when the police and medics arrived. They're not sure he's going to make it. They arrested her right on the spot. She confessed."

"She confessed? Wow."

"Mimi herself heard it and she told me. She says the police asked her what happened and she said I asked him if he slept with that slut and he said yes. So I axed him and axed him again."

"That's wild. I'm glad the girls didn't see any more than they did. Or me, either"

My mother had assured me that my sisters and I would be "safe and sound" living with Aunt CeCe. Did she know what kind of crazy building my aunt lived in?

32

A COUPLE OF WEEKS BEFORE CHRISTMAS, my father came home. I heard him and my mother talking. They were stressed and worried about having to provide for us for Christmas. Money was tight. My father, although he was feeling much better, wasn't able to work yet, and my mother had taken a lot of time off work—without pay—to go back and forth to Brockville to be with my father.

They were not in a good place and there wasn't a single thing I could do about it. Even though it wasn't my job to look after them and worry about them, that's the way I always felt. No choice. I was the "adult" in the family, wasn't I? I didn't sleep much over the next few nights. There was barely enough money for food, they were saying. There would be no Christmas gifts this year. My sisters would be devastated. I have to admit, so would I.

Two days before Christmas, we put up our tree and decorated it. I loved putting up the tree. My mother still had ornaments from her childhood. I loved asking her about them and listening to her talk about what it was like when she was a kid. She never seemed to mind talking about her childhood, such as it was. Every year, I would ask the same questions and, every year, my mother would answer them like she'd never been asked before. It was good to see her happy. It was good to have her talking to me about something.

I was in the kitchen finishing up the dishes when I heard a

commotion coming from the hall outside our apartment door. I figured it was the next door neighbor.

The voices and banging got louder. Then I realized one of the voices belonged to my mother. What was going on?

I quickly dried off my hands and went to the door to look out the peephole. My mother had boxes and other things in her arms and she was with two young men and a young woman whose arms were full, too. I didn't recognize these people, but I opened the door anyway.

Laughing, and calling out Merry Christmas, my mother stepped in. She set everything down, took off her coat, then collapsed in happiness and smiles on the couch.

The others returned with more boxes and placed them under the tree. Mother thanked them profusely, waving as they left.

"What's all this?" Would she answer me? Worth a shot to ask.

"Some of the staff at Eaton's pitched in and got us food. And gifts." She picked up a box and headed toward the kitchen with it.

"They bought stuff for *us*?" I wasn't sure I'd heard her right.

"Yep. We now have food for a few days. A couple of presents for you girls. It's wonderful, isn't it? We'll be able to have a good Christmas after all. I will definitely be counting my blessings tonight." She grabbed another box to unload. "And you should be, too."

I was speechless. I helped her unload the boxes and put everything away. My next job was to write "From Santa" on the gifts. They had already been wrapped in different colors. I couldn't wait to see what was in the boxes. My mother would hide them and put them under the tree on Christmas Eve.

I did count my blessings that night as I tried to control my excitement over this newfound knowledge: there were people out there. I was surprised, first of all, to realize there *were* people out there—I hadn't met many outside of school and family—but surprised mostly that there were people who cared about other people. That was a total shock. Completely out of my realm of experience.

Christmas morning, my sisters and I got up at our designated time, 5:00 AM.

We woke our parents. I had brought them each a cup of coffee. They sat on the couch to watch us open the gifts.

We always started with our stockings. We always got chocolate, candy canes and a Christmas orange.

But the gifts! Even a couple for my parents. Bubble bath for my mother and shaving stuff for my father.

I got clothes that I liked. (Finally!) I opened a box with New Kids on the Block items. There were other things, too. Wonderful things. My sisters were excited and happy.

It wasn't so much the gifts that were good, it was how I felt getting them. Getting them from people who cared about me. For the first time in my life, I felt like I mattered.

The food was yummy.

My parents got along.

Nothing was thrown.

It was the best Christmas I ever had.

I felt safe.

33

SHORTLY AFTER I STARTED MY first year of junior high, our family moved but we stayed in the same neighborhood, same school.

I had my own room once again. The building we had been living in was a series of buildings that were built in a rush to house people after WWII so they were meant to be temporary. As the years passed, housing was still needed so they remained, but the upkeep did not.

Eventually, the buildings began to violate building codes so it was decided it would be cheaper to demolish them and start over.

We moved to a big apartment building. We were lucky and ended up on the first floor which meant we had a small patio, plus, our apartment was two floors, like a house would be.

Life was looking better until the following week. I was now in junior high and there were no change rooms. I don't know where the boys got changed, but the girls changed inside a small storage area. You had to go up the stairs and turn right and there was a small space. I mean, we could fit ten of us, but like sardines. All the girls changed in front of everyone. That's just the way it was and there was no time to argue. I always tried to get undressed and dressed as fast as I could.

So this one day, I'm getting ready for gym. I'm with all the girls and everyone is chatting, talking about their latest crushes, their plans for the weekend, and the newest pimple—a real tragedy. Of course I wasn't chatting with anyone because I wasn't "popular." I had a couple of friends but they were not in my class.

I took off my pants, sweater, socks and shoes. There I stood in just my bra and white underwear.

If it hadn't been Chelsea, one of the most popular girls in the entire school, I might have been able to dampen the whole scene. But since it was Chelsea, I didn't have a hope from the word go. Teachers admired her, she was beautiful and smart (her father's being a diplomat helped), the boys adored her and would do whatever she asked or didn't ask them to do. No one wanted to get on Chelsea's bad side.

"Oh my gosh! Look at what Evie's wearing! She's wearing boys' underwear!" Chelsea said this loudly enough for everyone to hear and there she is, looking like a model in her matching bra and panties and pointing at me. I didn't even know you could buy a matching bra and panty set.

Within two seconds of Chelsea's opening her mouth, everyone's attention was on her and what she was going to say next. This was what happened every time Chelsea opened her mouth.

But to my horror, everyone turned to look at me instead. I wished the floor had opened up and swallowed me whole. I would never live this down.

"Look. She's wearing her brother's underwear!"

"I don't have a brother!" I yelled.

The giggling worsened.

Obviously, that had not been the right thing to say. But what else could I have said? It was true. I didn't have a brother.

The giggling stopped only when the gym teacher told us to get a move on and the girls rushed to get their gym stuff on and get down to the gym.

Not me. I turned away from them all to put my regular clothes back on. There was no way I was going down to the gym. There wasn't a doubt in my mind that Chelsea would tell all the boys in our class of the latest gossip involving me. There was no way I could face them.

I waited until I was the only one left in the change room. How could this happen?

I walked down the steps, down the hallway and out of the school. Once I was outside, the tears started. I had a good twenty blocks to walk home. I was used to it since I walked to and from school every day, no matter the weather. By block three, I was sobbing and needed tissues but didn't have any. Of course not.

By block five, I was wiping my nose on my sweater. I didn't care at this point.

By block ten, strangers were looking at me with wide eyes.

At block twelve, a stranger stopped to ask me if I was okay.

I did what any other normal teenager would do. I said "Yes," and started running.

At block sixteen, I had to stop to catch my breath.

By block eighteen, my tears were gone and my sweater was a complete mess.

By block nineteen, I hated my parents more than I ever thought possible.

I had figured out what happened.

A few days before this humiliating event, my mother had given me what she called "trendy new underwear." Six pairs. One of which I was now wearing.

I was thrilled. I had only two pairs and now I had eight. My parents rarely bought us clothes.

As it turned out, one of my mother's friends had bought these men's briefs for her husband and they were too small. My mother offered to take them. For me. What did I know? I'd never seen this type of underwear and my mother had told me it was the "latest trend."

I was the laughing stock of the entire school.

I was so mad at my mother, I actually told her about it.

She laughed, walked away and the subject was never spoken of again.

The only good news was that the incident happened on a Friday so I had the weekend to work up the courage to go back to school with the hope that the gossip had died down by then.

It hadn't.

But within a week—a week of hell—the giggling finally stopped.

34

I T WAS AFTER WE MOVED into the new apartment that things with my father got drastically worse. I was thirteen.

He woke me up in the middle of the night. "Evie," he whispered. "Get downstairs. Now."

I put on my bra, a T-shirt and slipped my legs into my jogging pants before I quickly ran downstairs. I already had my undies on. It must be some sort of emergency.

It was the middle of the night. Everyone else was sleeping. One small light was on.

My father was standing behind me. "Did you check to make sure the door was locked before you went to sleep?"

He was scaring me. I dared not say a word. That worked best when I had no idea what my father was talking about.

I never checked the door before I went to bed. My parents went to bed long after I did. Didn't they make sure everything was locked? Why was this my job? Yet again, my job to do something adult?

"What about the windows? Did you check if they were locked before you went to bed?" Was he actually grinding his teeth in anger?

I had no idea what was going on. I couldn't even smell alcohol on him. Everything felt wrong. Very wrong. Something bad was going to happen. I wanted to bolt, but I couldn't move.

Suddenly, he grabbed me. Violently. He dragged me to the door.

"Check it. Make sure it's locked."

Shaking, I made sure the door was locked. Next, he dragged me to the two living room windows. I checked the first one. It was locked. I checked the second window. It was locked. The same with the back door, between the windows.

What next?

"You know why you need to make sure the windows and doors are locked, Evie?"

I could feel the tears coming but I bit my bottom lip. I would not allow myself to cry.

"Because a man could come inside, grab you and rape you."

Roughly, he spun me around to face him. "Take off your clothes."

I didn't move. This wasn't my father. This was some kind of monster. This was a dream. I pinched myself. Right on the arm. I did. I actually pinched myself, hoping to wake up. It didn't work.

He grabbed my wrist and shook me. It hurt.

"I said, take off your clothes."

I slowly removed my jogging pants. His eyes never left me.

"Keep going. We don't have all night."

I closed my eyes and took off my T-shirt, hoping that would be the end of whatever sick game he was playing. I let my shirt drop to the carpet.

"You aren't done yet."

Was this real? I was so scared, I could barely stay on my feet. I was sure my stomach was going to hurl its contents at him—thinking back, I wonder if that would have made a difference—or that I'd pass out right there, right on the floor.

I took off my undies then my bra. I tried to cover myself by putting my hands over my breasts, but he pulled them away.

"You got to learn. You got to remember to check the doors and windows so no one breaks in and rapes you."

He began to pace the living room. Not once did I think of screaming or calling out to my mother. I was too scared.

Then he lunged at me and grabbed my nipples and squeezed and squeezed and squeezed until I collapsed from the pain.

When I came to, he was gone. I managed to get myself to my bedroom. The rest of the night I couldn't sleep. I kept thinking he was coming back for me. Even to this day, I have trouble sleeping sometimes. Some days, when the moon is in a certain phase maybe, or when something triggers a memory about locks or windows and doors, I can't sleep.

The next morning my father smiled and asked me how I was doing.

Every night after that, I always made sure both the front and back doors were locked along with both windows in the living room.

It didn't make any difference. He didn't stop. This was only the beginning.

35

ONE EVENING, A FEW MONTHS after the original incident, I was at home with my father. Just the two of us. I knew that work had been slowing down for him because he was home more often now. Again.

I heard the shower running. I breathed a sigh of relief knowing I was safe for a while, at least. I was avoiding my father as much as possible. Life had become unbearable never knowing when he was going to strike next. I couldn't sleep at night because I kept wondering when he would come for me. I couldn't tell anyone. My mother wouldn't believe me, or even worse, she'd *blame* me. I didn't know how else I could handle it.

I couldn't handle the pain and all the secrets anymore. It was too much. All I thought about now was my father and ways I could end my own life.

After the first time, I wrote a suicide letter. I took a steak knife and tried to slice my left wrist open. I did a crappy job of that, barely drawing any blood at all. I bandaged myself up and shredded the note before anyone saw it and I got in trouble for it. Mustn't ever make my parents look bad to others.

The shower was still running so I was caught off guard when he was suddenly right beside me.

I tried to step away from him, but he grabbed my arm.

"Have you ever let anyone touch you?"

I shook my head no. Why was the shower running if there was no one in it?

"Liar." He dragged me toward the bathroom and flung open the door and tossed me into the freezing cold shower.

I struggled to get out but he held me in the cold flow, calling me a liar over and over.

What was he was talking about? Water was getting into my mouth. I was having trouble breathing. Was he trying to drown me?

The more I struggled, the more he seemed to enjoy himself.

I stopped fighting. This was no way to live.

I don't know how long this went on. I zoned out.

He finally shut the water off and yanked me out of the tub, out of the bathroom, into the hallway.

I was completely drenched and shivering with cold. I had never been so cold. I wrapped my arms around my body, hoping for warmth. It didn't work. I needed to get out of my wet clothes.

He stood there staring at me, looking me up and down.

"Get undressed. Take your clothes off."

I lowered my head. I would resist this time.

He smacked me.

I took off my clothes.

He disappeared into his bedroom and came out with his leather belt and something else. A metal buckle.

I was completely naked.

He attached the metal buckle to the belt.

He smiled.

The belt struck me on the left butt cheek.

On the right butt cheek.

I screamed each time the belt struck.

He turned me and whipped the belt across my stomach.

I bent over with the pain.

I screamed.

Over and over and over and over I screamed.

I begged him to stop but he wouldn't.

The buckle struck my breasts. Over and over.

I lost count then. I didn't know where he was hitting me anymore. Just that he was. Over and over and over.

Then he stopped.

He picked up my wet clothes, flung them at me and walked away.

I crawled to my room where I passed out on my bed.

The next day, I threw those clothes out.

36

S OMETIMES, ON A WEEKEND, MY friend, Sonya (yes, I finally had a best friend) would ask me to help her deliver papers. In return, she'd treat me to McDonald's, or sometimes something else.

Sonya was at least twice my size, which meant no one messed with her, which meant I felt safe with her. I had spent the night at her house several times. On this particular night, we were having a pajama party, just the two of us.

"Let's get into our pajamas. We can listen to Marky Mark and the Funky Bunch while we're doing it. Snacks with the movie? Okay, Evie?"

It sounded good to me. There were lots of things I liked about being at Sonya's house. Her mother was super nice and her father didn't live with them. By now, I didn't trust adult males. Sonya's place was quiet, there was plenty of food. Her mother never complained when we took snacks to Sonya's room. Sonya didn't have to ask permission. She just took what she wanted. Whatever food we had in my house, we always had to ask permission. Beg for it? That went for everything except for water. At least we were allowed water. But that depended on the time of day. After school, it would "fill us up" so we wouldn't eat supper and be "annoying our parents for food later." Or we'd be "up all night going pee," disturbing their sleep.

I liked Sonya. She could have told me to do anything and I would have done it just so she would keep me as a friend.

"Sounds good to me, Sonya. I'll go get changed in the bathroom."

"Seriously, Evie? I don't understand what the big deal is. Just get changed here with me."

I didn't know what to do. I wanted her to stay friends with me. So, despite my lack of self-confidence and without thinking, I took off my pants and shirt. I stood in her room wearing just my bra and underwear.

She had her back to me and had taken off her clothes as well. She was in her bra and underwear, too. She was a big girl but her weight didn't bother her. I would have liked to have even *half* the self-confidence she had.

I heard her say something but I couldn't make out what. "Pardon? I didn't hear you."

Sonya turned around to face me and was about to repeat herself when her eyes widened. She took three quick steps to close the space between us. She pointed.

"What the hell happened? Who did that to you?"

Gently, she turned me to examine my legs, my butt—the cuts went beyond the edge of my panties—my abdomen and my chest.

Damn it. I'd been having so much fun with Sonya, I'd forgotten about the cuts and bruises. I was still sore, but it wasn't as bad as when it had first happened.

I didn't know what to tell her. I didn't want to lose her as a friend but I had to say something. I *had* to say something.

"It's nothing. I fell off my bike." I smiled.

"Evie, you don't have a bike. And you don't look like that when you fall off a bike. Who did this to you?"

She handed me my clothes so I could put them back on. Then she put her arms around me and drew me in close. At her touch, I couldn't take it anymore and started sobbing.

We sat on her bed until my tears subsided.

There would be no listening to music or watching a movie. She did get us snacks, though.

I had to tell someone. I couldn't hold on to the hurt that was locked inside me anymore. All I had been thinking about was ways to end my life. I was a walking zombie because of the nightmares when I did sleep, but I was more afraid *to* sleep in case the monster came for me again. By now, I'd lost track of the number of times it had happened. There was even a time he woke me up in the middle of the night and the doors and windows *were* unlocked—even though I *had* locked them before going to bed.

No matter what I did, he wouldn't stop.

"It's your father isn't it?" asked Sonya. "He's the one who did it, isn't it?" She pounded her fist on the bed.

I didn't answer her but I think my sobs told her *yes*.

"Was this because of the make-up incident?"

I couldn't bring myself to tell her about what he was doing to my breasts. That this had been going on for months. I couldn't. I'd let her think it was related to the make-up incident. So I told her about the make-up incident instead.

The make-up incident? I had been given permission from my father to wear make-up. The only rule was, I had to go see someone who specialized in make-up so they could show me how to apply it properly and tell me what colors looked good on me. "To make sure I didn't end up like I was going out for a night of hooking on the street." My father's exact words.

It was Sonya who took me to see the girl at the make-up counter. I listened to everything the girl said and I picked out mascara, foundation, tinted lip gloss and eyeliner.

I was going out to meet friends that night. I put on my make-up just the way the girl at the make-up counter had told me to, "Less is always more. You need to make it look like it's all natural beauty. All you." I wasn't even wearing eyeliner because I couldn't figure that one out yet. I had given my lashes a few swipes of mascara and had applied tinted lip gloss.

The problem was, my father was home. When I headed for the door to leave, he called out. "Where the hell do you think you're going?"

"The basketball court. With my friends."

That's where all us teens hung out. That's where I always hung out. This wasn't news to my father .

"Not dressed like that you're not!"

I looked down at what I was wearing. A printed flower turtle neck my mother had bought for back-to-school, black hand-me-down jeans, shoes, and my hair was pulled back in a clip. And the make-up.

I stared at him. What was he talking about? Was he joking? (Even though he rarely did.)

He walked away from me, went upstairs and headed straight for my room. I could hear his footsteps.

By the time I got there, he had gathered up all my new make-up—over a month's worth of babysitting money—was in the bathroom down the hall, had put the plug in the bathroom sink and, as it was filling up with water, had dumped all my make-up into it.

"You said I could. I asked before I bought this stuff. I worked hard so I could buy it. I did everything you told me to do and it still wasn't good enough?"

He slapped me hard across the face.

I went to my room and shut my door and as I did, I heard my father yelling, "You're nothing but a whore!"

37

A WEEK OR SO AFTER THE pajama party, such as it had ended up to be, I was in the change room. Gym class was over. Nothing bad had happened. *Yes,* I said to myself. *It was going to be a good day.*

But as usual, I was wrong. Would there ever be such a thing as a good day in Evie Feather's life? Could I ever do anything right?

I was in the middle of wrapping my purple scrunchie around my pony tail when the school intercom blasted out, "Evie Feathers. Please come to the office."

All the girls looked my way.

I shrugged, then made my way down the office. I was in trouble for something. *No matter what, don't argue,* I told myself. That way, I could get it over with as soon as possible. That worked at home, why not at school?

The secretary nodded at me but didn't smile. Now I was really worried.

I knocked on the door to the principal's office.

Mr. Fung opened it right away and told me to come in. To sit.

At first I thought it was just the two of us in the office. Don't forget, I had trained myself not to see what I didn't want to see.

I heard the door shut behind me.

It was then, from the corner of my eye—and don't forget, I had trained myself to be on constant alert for anyone sneaking up on me, too—that I saw the two police officers. One was male and one was female. And there was a second female, not in a uniform. They were staring at me.

My first instinct was to run but I reminded myself that the door was shut and there were cops only a few feet from me. I sighed. I waited.

But cops? I'd never dealt with the police before. My parents wouldn't just beat me, they would actually kill me for this. Whatever this was.

Mr. Fung's face became soft and kind as he leaned toward me. "Evie? These police officers would like to talk to you. Is that okay with you?"

I almost laughed out loud. Like I had a choice. "Sure."

What was going on? I couldn't think of anything I'd done wrong. Maybe someone I knew was in trouble and they wanted to see if I had any information. I tried to think of who it could be. It was probably someone from my neighborhood. Yes. That could be it. Or… Could it be Sonya? She'd been in trouble before for shoplifting. Maybe she'd done it again. Or maybe she'd been caught and had implicated me.

Now that I was making up imaginary scenarios, the ugly feeling in the pit of my stomach was dissipating. Now I was just angry. As if I didn't have enough to deal with. How could she do this to me?

As it turned out, she hadn't done anything *to* me, she had done something *for* me.

38

THE DAY AFTER SONYA FOUND out about my father, she had gone to see Holly, her own counselor.

"Why do you want to see me today?" Holly asked. "Usually you make an appointment. Is there something in particular you need to tell me? Did something happen? Something serious?"

"It's not about me. Things are good with me. Things are better with my mom, so that's good. It's just... See. I have this friend..."

Holly's eyes searched Sonya's. Counselors are well aware of the "asking for a friend" ruse that people often resort to in order to talk about something difficult.

"And I found out this weekend, that something bad is happening to her. I need to know what I can do to help her."

"I see. How about you tell me more about what's going on with this friend. The more I know, the easier it will be to help her."

"Something has to be done right away. She's really scared. She's hurting. Inside and out. There are even marks all over her body."

Holly sat up higher. "Marks?"

"I don't want to give you a name. I don't want to upset her. She was at my place this weekend. We had a sleepover. We were dancing around and listening to music. Then it started to get late so I suggested we change into our pajamas. Watch a movie."

Sonya paused.

"Continue, Sonya. It's okay. We'll figure this out."

"Well, we weren't facing each other or anything but we started changing. I said something to her and she didn't hear me and she turned around to ask me to repeat what I said. I turned around and I saw the marks. She had bruises and other marks all over the place. On her chest, like, on her boobs, y'know? What I could see of her boobs. She had a bra on. The marks were on her legs, too. Everywhere. As soon as she saw that I saw, she covered up. I couldn't exactly ask to see more. I asked her if it was her father and she started crying. I'm sure it's her father doing it. He's really mean. He yells at her all the time."

There. It was out. She had told someone.

"You should be very proud of yourself, Sonya. I know it wasn't easy to talk to me about this. Give yourself a pat on the back. We'll work this through. It's going to be okay. Make an appointment with my receptionist for next week. If you need anything before then, don't hesitate to call."

As soon as Sonya left her office and had shut the door, Holly opened Sonya's file and dialed the number there. She would speak to Sonya's mother. She would find out what was going on. Someone was hurting Sonya. Or hurting someone close to her.

39

THE MALE POLICE OFFICER SPOKE first. "We received an anony-mous call regarding your well-being. Your situation at home?"

This was definitely not good and had nothing to do with Sonya shoplifting or anything else. This was about me. There was no way this was going to turn out good. I was screwed. What was I going to do or say? I waited for them to read me my rights. I knew I had the right to keep silent.

The female officer tried. "Evie? Is someone at home hurting you? You can tell us. It's okay. It's our job to make sure everyone is safe."

Seriously? If this was, in fact, their "job," where had they been my entire life? Obviously, this was a lie. Maybe my parents were testing me? That would make sense. According to my father, what happens in the house stays in the house. Everybody knows that. Don't they?

I would use strategy. I'd answer a question with a question. This would give me more time to think.

"What do you mean? I don't understand."

The lady who wasn't in a uniform spoke up. "Is anyone at home, anyone who lives with you, hitting you, touching you inappropriately, or not treating you properly?"

I said nothing. I had the right to be silent. And even if I didn't have the right to be silent, my father would beat me senseless if he found out I'd said anything. *What happens in the house, stays in the house.*

"Does your father or mother or someone else in your home hit you with their hands or with anything else?"

I closed my eyes. I wanted everyone in the room to disappear. I wanted to disappear. This was another of those many times I wished I were only three inches tall. They wouldn't be able to catch me if I ran.

Mr. Fung spoke next. "The police know something is going on. They need to hear it from you. There are no right or wrong answers. You just need to tell the truth."

The truth? I almost laughed. Nothing had ever gotten me in trouble *more* than telling the truth. But it didn't look like they were going to let me leave anytime soon. Once again, I had no choice.

"Okay. Um. Sometimes my father hits me with his hands. And. Um. A few times he hit me with his leather belt. With the buckle end."

I closed my eyes, waiting for lightning to strike. Or my father's fist from somewhere out of the air. I'd broken the sacred rule of our household: *What happens in the house, stays in the house. It's nobody's business but ours.* I had told the truth. My father was going to kill me.

The lady without the uniform was taking notes and so was the female police officer.

The male officer and Mr. Fung locked eyes, communicating with one another without using actual words. I knew all about how that worked. My parents had taught me how to read their thoughts long ago. I never messed that one up.

Half of me was wondering when I could go back to class and the other half of me was wondering if should save everyone the trouble and run away.

The lady without the uniform said, "Evie? My name is Helen. You're going to come with me and we're going to go somewhere quiet so we can talk. I'll come with you to your locker. We'll get anything you need to bring with you."

She then spoke quietly to Mr. Fung then to each of the police officers.

What had she said? We were leaving? I had classes.

I silently prayed the police would not follow me to my locker. I'd been through enough already. If the other kids saw cops at my locker, I'd have to switch schools for sure. No way they'd let something like that go. They'd dig and dig and dig and wouldn't stop harassing me until I told them something. That's the way my schoolmates were.

I was thankful that both police officers stayed in the office with the principal. But they'd left the office door open.

As Helen and I walked down the hall toward my locker, some kids and a couple of the teachers were watching from open doors. Did they know? Once at my locker, I was so nervous, it took me four tries to get my combination right.

I grabbed my bag.

We checked in again at the office.

I left the school with Helen close by my side. Did she think I was going to run or something?

I would have if I'd had some place to go.

***

I'm not sure where I thought we were going. My place? No. We pulled up at the police station. Why? I hadn't done anything wrong. Maybe according to my father I had, but nothing against the law. Not that I knew of anyway.

"We'll talk here. Then we'll go grab something to eat. If you like." She smiled.

The food part sounded great but what was there to talk about? I didn't want to talk about my shitty home life anymore. *Living* through it had been enough. Let's not *re*live it in front of strangers.

Helen and I sat alone in a room. I guess her job was to get me talking and then the police would take it from there.

She wanted to know how many times my father had hit me, what he had used, had he tried to touch me, and many other things I wanted to forget.

It was hard to explain, I told her. I'd lost track of how many times he'd laid his hands on me, I said.

Honestly, it had been going on so long, I didn't know where to start.

They weren't going to let me go until I talked. No choice.

The worst of it had been over the last several months. That's where I decided to start. I would start at my father's suicide attempt. I would tell her it was like something inside of him snapped. I'd say he just wasn't the same person. No matter what I did or how I did it was always wrong according to my father. That way, my father wouldn't be so angry with me. I was defending him. Wasn't I?

Helen and I had been chatting for a while before the female police officer came in and gave us some "incident forms" to fill out.

I would have to relive each "incident" that had taken place in the last few months and write it out in as much detail as I could, they said.

It took hours. Hours on the actual clock and they just kept bringing me more paper. But Helen was at my side the entire time and even came with me to the bathroom once. I felt like a prisoner. But I knew they couldn't keep me there. I was going to be fourteen soon.

After filling out each sheet, I had to sign it. I don't remember how many full sheets of eight-by-fourteen-inch paper I used. I stopped counting after ten.

Then. I was finally done. Finally done telling stuff that was supposed to be kept a secret. I was in big trouble. Huge trouble.

The police were satisfied, they said, satisfied that I had told them every single secret of our house. I hadn't, of course. I'd merely given them enough to make them stop asking, "Is there anything else you want to add?"

I signed the last sheet of paper. I was finally finished.

"What's going to happen now, Helen? I can't go home. Not after this. He'll kill me for sure." My voice was shaking. Tears were sitting there waiting. Until then, I'd held together pretty well but the thought of going home was too much.

"I'm going to drive you home. Don't worry. Your father will not be there. You'll be safe. No one can hurt you anymore."

She let me finish my cheeseburger and fries even though she knew I was eating them as slowly as I possibly could to put off the inevitable.

No. This was just a bad dream. A bad dream while awake. I was experienced with those. Really experienced with those.

***

As Helen neared my place, two police cars passed but stayed ahead of us.

Deep down, I knew where they were going but I asked anyway, "They're not going to my place, are they? Those police? Are they going to my place?"

"They're going to talk to your father."

He was the last person I wanted to see. I was terrified. He would kill me on sight. Cops or no cops.

"If they're arresting him, I don't want to be there. I don't want to be there. I couldn't handle it. Please. Make sure he doesn't see me!"

"Everything's going to be fine, Evie. Everything's going to be fine."

As she slowed down in front of our place, four police officers were taking my father away. His hands were cuffed. Two officers were behind him and two others were holding his arms. I prayed he wouldn't look in my direction. At least that small blessing was granted to me. He looked straight ahead, never in my direction.

In a neighborhood like ours, word spreads fast when cop cars pull up in front of somebody's residence. People were even sitting on their front steps. Others were gathering around Helen's car. Some of them knew I was the daughter of the man being arrested. It felt as though everyone in the entire *city* was watching—not just watching him, but watching me, too. We were both being watched. Judged! I was surprised nobody was eating popcorn! What would it be like in the gym's change room at school?

Stories of why Gabe Feathers had been arrested buzzed around the neighborhood for several days. Some stories were worse or less than I might have imagined. Some were not so far from the truth.

Main thing: He hadn't seen me.

But I wanted it all to go away. I needed it all to go away.

I turned my eyes down to look at the floor of Helen's car. Spotless. Even the little garbage bag hanging from the glove compartment was empty.

Then I couldn't hold it in any longer. The tears flowed. Tears of sorrow? Tears of fear? Guilt? Relief?

Suppressed rage?

My father was charged with sexual interference, sexual assault, assault with a weapon, assault causing bodily harm…

He told my mother he didn't want to put me through the "ordeal of a court trial"—me? Daddy was thinking of *me* all of a sudden?—so that's why he decided to plead guilty? Wasn't it also to make sure this "little issue" was kept quiet and out of the public, Daddy? His pleading guilty also caused the Crown to drop half the charges.

My father ruined my life and got two years probation for it. Free as a bird and I was still caged in the basement of my mind.

40

M Y MOTHER WOULDN'T SPEAK TO me. I could feel her hatred burning into the back of my neck every time I entered the room she was in. It took her weeks to calm down. I guess she realized we both lived in the same house? So let's keep it as peaceful as possible?

She never asked me what had happened. I don't know if she saw the documents I'd filled out and signed at the police station. After I left home the night of the beer bottle incident, when I was seventeen, the night my father threatened to kill me, she fabricated the story that I ran away from home because they wouldn't extend my curfew. Family members believed her. I wouldn't doubt she'd make up something about this, too. In my father's favor.

My father has a physical scar from the night of the beer bottle incident. How it happened was enough to make me start believing in Karma. He had smashed the beer bottle but as he was coming at me with a chunk of it, he stepped on top of the rest of the broken glass. A two-inch piece of beer bottle pierced the inside of his left ankle and lodged there. He should have gone to the hospital, but how would he explain that one?

I was gone, of course, but my mother told my sister Dee Dee later how he'd taken care of it. My mother had seemed proud of him, Dee Dee told me. What he did was chug down two more beer and then went to work on giving himself first aid. He soaked his foot in bleach, pulled out the glass, and even gave himself stitches. A brave man like that could never have done anything that his daughter accused him of. Could he? Never.

Another thing making my life difficult the year I was "almost fourteen" was that after he was arrested, every time I ran into someone from my neighborhood, they'd pretend to be my friend so I'd maybe tell them what happened. They all wanted to know when my father was coming back, they'd say. I ignored them.

The saddest part of it all, I think, is that Sonya and I stopped hanging out. I'm not sure why. Perhaps we were both no longer the same people. Maybe it was "time to move on" as they say in the movies and on TV. Years later, I ran into her at a bingo hall but she didn't seem to really care about chatting with me. It's like she wanted to forget. So I obliged her. I could understand. I wanted to forget, too.

41

AFTER RUNNING AWAY FROM HOME that night when I was seven-teen, I stayed with a friend. A week later, I got a part-time job downtown working at a deli. Two weeks after that, I was going to school full-time again, and working part time. It was my last year of high school and I was determined to graduate. My parents had not. There was no way I wanted to be anything like them if I could do something about it.

The first month out on my own went well. I was paying rent and was on top of everything. Two months after leaving home, I had my own one-bedroom apartment. I had friends at school now because everyone thought it was neat that I had my own apartment. I was working and had no one to answer to but myself. Yeah, it was exciting. But eventually the excitement wore off. I didn't always make the best decisions. Had I inherited that from my father? Or had I just learned that from never being able to practice?

There was the time I went out with the girls from work to get a tattoo. No thinking involved. It was a spur of the moment kind of thing. After all, I lived on my own now. I could do whatever I wanted because there was no one to stop me. My parents couldn't ground me. I was the one who made the choices and I was the one who suffered the consequences.

While my friend was getting her tattoo, I picked one out for myself.

No real thought. I don't recommend doing that. Ever. I picked out a cute tattoo, a pair of cherries. I figured it could go on my lower thigh. When I had lived at home, I'd always wanted to wear a bikini but was not allowed because that would make me a whore according to my father. So of course I had the tattoo done. I would buy a bikini to show it off, too.

Then there was the time I dyed my hair jet black and took up smoking cigarettes because I wanted to fit in with my friends. My skin tone looked horrible with black hair. Everyone kept asking me if I was sick. A rumor actually started going around the school that I was terminally ill and putting on a brave face because I didn't want anyone to know. The smoking lasted for only three months. My friends sat me down for an intervention for that one. I didn't inhale and was only smoking a pack of cigarettes a week but still, it was in my best interests to quit, they said. Wow. Somebody actually cared about me.

Then there was the time I had a party at my place. The next morning I got only as far as two steps outside my bedroom door before I stopped in my tracks. On the living room floor were about a dozen people, most of them still sleeping. Four were awake and chatting. That must have been what woke me up. Two of the four were complete strangers to me. The other two I knew. The longer I stood there, taking in the scene, the wilder it looked. This was not my imagination at work. There were empty bottles of beer, alcohol and other garbage all over my living room floor.

I was barefoot. I took a step forward. Unexpectedly, my right foot slipped in something gooey and I fell. I laughed. Everyone did.

When the laugher died down, I got up to see what I had slipped on. To my horror, it was a pile of condoms. Not *a* condom. Several. Used ones. I had slipped on a pile of used condoms and landed on them. My stomach didn't give me time to make it to the bathroom. I threw up all over my living room floor.

That was it.

"Get out of my house now. You have ten minutes to get your crap and leave. If anyone is still here in ten minutes, I'll call the cops."

"Hey, MAP. You need to chill," a guy yelled back.

"Who are you talking to?"

"You. The loudmouth. Freaking over nothing. Jeez."

"My name is Evie, not Map. Get out." I took several threatening steps toward him. (At least I'd learned one beneficial thing from my father: how to threaten people.)

Within ten minutes, everyone except for my two friends, had cleared out.

I couldn't believe this. My friends let me cry while they cleaned up some of the garbage in my living room. When I had collected myself, I pitched in, too. It took the three of us over an hour to get my apartment back in shape. I hopped into the shower.

When I came out of the bathroom there were two large pizzas and pop waiting. We ate together and my friends spent the night.

***

A couple of days later, the guy who had given me attitude at my place—shall I call him Dick?—showed up in one of my classes. I didn't think anything of it at the time. However, by the end of the week, he had transferred into every single one of my classes. It was creepy. I spoke to someone in the guidance office at school but they weren't sympathetic. They listened, but according to them, Dick wasn't doing anything wrong. That was true. He hadn't done anything.

Yet.

The day after I complained to the school, I came home to find my cat—who always came in at night, then left again in the morning—dead at my apartment door. I knew it was Dick who had done it.

My dead cat was the last straw. I went to the school's office and demanded they do something. I had a meeting with the school's social worker, and the principal.

After much debate, it was decided it would be best if I moved to another school. The guy does this to me and kills my cat and *I* am the one who has to make the changes in *my* life? I didn't want to but now, we were talking about my safety.

After I changed schools, my friends stopped calling. That told me it was time to start thinking about what I wanted to do with my life instead of making impulsive decisions. I was pissed off, but most of all, I was disappointed in myself. How could I have let this happen? I had fallen off the path and it was time to move forward. So I did.

I continued working part time.

I finished the last of my high-school courses. I graduated.

I went to college and graduated.

I got married.

I had children.

I got divorced.

Life went on. The path was sometimes bumpy but at least I was on my own road, wasn't I?

Epilogue

IT WASN'T EVEN 7:00 AM that Saturday morning. I opened one eye to peek at my alarm clock. I stared at the time for a full minute watching the numbers click by, but the time didn't miraculously change back so I could sleep longer.

There never seemed to be enough hours in a day anymore. There was always so much to do. That was the concrete thing about time. Once you willingly—or unwillingly—spent it, it couldn't be taken back. It was gone for good. I had already missed out on so much, there was no more time to waste.

I shook my head trying to clear the dream cobwebs away. There had to be a reason I had set the alarm for such a ridiculously early time on a Saturday. I closed my eyes and silently counted to ten. The reason was on the tip of my tongue. Abby! That's right. I had to meet my daughter, Abby, at half past eight. We were meeting at the University of Ottawa. Abby was currently in her last year of high school. Applications and deadlines loomed. Abby needed to narrow down her choices. A couple of days earlier, Abby had sent a text asking if I would go with her to listen to the various presentations at the university. The presentations, she told me, would help her narrow down her choices for her program and major.

I gently nudged Trent, my partner of nearly two years, who was sleeping peacefully beside me. No response. I nudged him again. I considered letting him sleep then decided against that because he'd said he wanted to go with us.

"Are you sure you want to come with me? You can stay here and catch a couple more hours of sleep. I don't mind, really."

Trent rolled over, stretched and smiled. Our eyes locked. How I loved his ocean blue eyes. How had I gotten so lucky? After dealing with guys who didn't put much thought into anything, Trent was a welcome change.

"We could go to the Rideau mall at lunch break," he said. "Grab a bite. Maybe look around if you girls are up for it."

What a sweetheart. Early on a Saturday morning and he was going to come with us to the open house.

No matter how well I tried to plan things out, I was always scurrying around until the very last minute. Then it was rush, rush, rush. I was constantly telling Trent, that next time, I would be more organized. Trent, who never seemed to run out of patience, was the complete opposite. He was always organized and could locate anything within thirty seconds.

It was a couple of minutes past eight. Neither Trent nor I had had anything to eat yet and I was missing my coffee. This was not a good way to start out early on an academic morning. I should have been up earlier making coffee instead of watching the minutes tick by on the clock. There. See? I still had this habit of blaming myself for everything. That I was responsible for everything. That everything that went wrong was my fault. But I was working on it. I even laughed at myself sometimes now when I caught myself doing it.

"We need to leave for the bus in like two minutes at the most," Trent reminded me.

I double checked that I had enough change for the bus fare.

Trent had a pass.

***

I didn't get to see my daughter as much as I would have liked. She had recently moved in her with her father to have more room and be closer to everything. She had a part-time job working at the grocery store and she played on a Frisbee team.

Then there she was. My daughter, Abby. Smiling, she walked toward us. We hugged as soon as we were close enough to do so. I couldn't believe how grown up she looked.

The three of us walked side by side and kept chatting as we made our way to the nearest information booth. According to Abby, we needed to locate the Social Sciences building. At least Abby's presentations were all in the same building. This pretty much erased the chances of getting lost and of Abby's missing anything important.

Abby and I grabbed more information pamphlets, a really cool, branded, school pen, then made our way farther into the school. I suddenly stopped in awe. I stared down at the huge University of Ottawa logo. It was white and was set against the pale gray carpet. It seemed so posh, for some reason it spoke to me.

"What, Mom?"

"Nothing."

What I could I say? I couldn't believe this was really happening. My daughter was going to university! This was real. It wasn't in my imagination, something I'd dreamed up to make real life go away. It was real.

Of course, this feeling was not completely new. I'd had the same emotional reaction when I'd attended a college open house with Abby's older brother, my son Christian, to check out different computer programs he'd wanted to apply for.

I shook my head and told myself it was perfectly normal for a parent to have these moments. It was a very proud and important moment to have a teen heading off to college or university—even a college or university that was in the same city. Off into The Real

World, a place I'd never been allowed to go to as a child.

That was the thing, though. I didn't feel that I was a normal parent, living in a normal world. The entire time I was raising my children, I'd had no idea what I was doing, so constantly feared, that at any moment, they would be taken away from me. That was my biggest fear. I was only eighteen when Christian was born, a child myself.

Where had the time gone? Decades, hours, pivotal moments had all rushed through my life's kaleidoscope and in the end, they were captured in just a few moments into something that took my breath away with its beauty.

I had to restrain myself from taking out my cell phone to snap pictures of that carpet. I mean, really, I was trying to blend in with this exciting moment for Abby. The last thing I wanted to do was embarrass her. I knew only too well what that was like. No matter what it took, I had to give my children everything they needed. That's how it was supposed to be. I tried to give my children the tools required to make it. My children should not have to pay for the choices my parents had made. Or the decisions I made, either.

We made our way to the Psychology presentation room. The seats were split up into three sections, left, middle and right. About two dozen students were already seated. It would start in a few minutes. I wasn't sure what to do and I didn't want to be noticed so, taking in every detail, as was my usual, I headed for the far right of the room. There was not a single student or parent on the far right side, making it the perfect location for us, in my opinion.

Abby sat to my left and Trent sat on my right. We would stay for this presentation and for the one after.

I had been under the impression that a presentation would have a person at the front of the room who did all the talking. Apparently, this was not that kind of presentation. This speaker, a guest, asked questions and he expected parents and students to raise their hands with answers.

Abby volunteered to answer questions three times. I'm sure that wasn't easy to do in a room full of strangers, but she did it and I was proud.

After the second presentation was over, we all walked the ten minutes to the local mall to grab lunch and walk around. As we ate at the food court, we discussed the different programs. Abby, as yet, hadn't decided what she wanted to major or even minor in. She was definitely applying to a couple of different programs, though, but needed to narrow down her selections and make, what she called, "a plan of attack." Brave girl. So unlike me at her age.

After lunch, we said our goodbyes. Abby had at least one more presentation after lunch but was meeting a friend. They would go together.

It had been great seeing Abby. I remembered years ago, when she'd had hardly any hair, and now it was down to her waist. After having Christian, I wanted a girl, then, too. When I had Abby, I couldn't wait to put little pigtails and bows in her hair, not the elastics that had been put in mine.

Gone were those days. I couldn't believe how fast they were growing up. And how well their lives were turning out.

Their childhoods had been completely different from mine. How lucky they were to have had a mother—*me*, if I could believe it—who had wanted to stop the downhill snowball of addiction and narcissistic abuse from striking yet another generation. I had succeeded.

***

Just as I was about to unlock the door to my place, I realized that Abby and I had not taken any selfies of our university adventure. That made me sad. But I didn't cry. I was learning that crying wasn't always from sadness. That it was mostly from frustration. I was working on that one, too. Learn the reason. Address it. Fixed.

At least it would be a nice, quiet evening with Trent. It was Halloween and my kids were off doing their own thing. Gone were the days where the kids bugged and bugged me, I swear, every single minute wanting to know how many more sleeps until Halloween, and changing their mind about their costumes after discussing different options with their friends. And they *had* friends.

Despite my negative childhood experiences, I had kept one Halloween tradition going from my past.

My parents never bought fancy, decorated Halloween buckets or bags for us to take trick-or-treating. We always used a pillowcase. Back then, I thought it was strange, but the neighborhood kids always thought it was an original idea. The pillowcases never broke; they didn't melt if they got wet in the rain; and they could be slung over our shoulders when the weight of the candy increased as we left each block behind us. There was always enough room in the bags as well. It was nice to have learned at least one beneficial thing from my parents.

When trick-or-treating was done with my own kids for the night, we'd go home and they'd take off the parts of the costumes that were annoying: masks, headpieces or make-up. I would order in pizza and then we'd sort the candy while we waited for supper to arrive. By 7:30 PM the kids' stomachs would be full, they'd be in pajamas, and all the candy would have been checked. Then it was scary TV shows until it was time for bed.

***

This particular Halloween evening, Trent ordered in the pizza and started through the list of scary movies for us to watch. First up was *Chucky*, then *Edward Scissorhands* and then *Arachnophobia*. Believe it or not, not a single trick-or-treater knocked on our door. I was glad. I didn't really want to see cute kids dressed up as Elsa or Iron Man or Minnie Mouse. It would be yet another reminder of how fast my kids had grown up, and how much older I was getting.

When the kids were younger, I couldn't wait until they were no longer on the bottle, no longer using a soother, and no longer needing diapers or pull-ups. Then I couldn't wait until they started school so I could have a mug of coffee without having to reheat it a dozen times. Then it was like time went on fast-forward. I couldn't stop it.

I won't ever forget the day I was applying foundation to my face and while I spread it below one of my eyes, I saw a white hair. This white hair wasn't on my head, though. That would seem normal. Appropriate. This particular white hair was an actual eyelash. An eyelash! That couldn't be normal. What could I do? What should I do? What would I do? Now that I knew it was there, I couldn't just let it mock me. It would be only a matter of time before other people noticed it. I couldn't have that, could I? I needed to get rid of it. And fast. The smart thing to do would be look up this crisis on Google. See what other people might suggest. But that would take time and I wanted it gone. Like, yesterday.

I decided to take care of this myself.

I grabbed my trusty tweezers and slowly leaned toward the medicine cabinet's mirror.

In my haste to make myself look younger, I banged my forehead on the mirror. Instinctively, I glanced behind me in case someone—my mother? my father?—had noticed my incompetence.

All clear.

Then I leaned forward again to peer more closely at the person in the mirror. The "person" in the mirror? That wasn't a person. That was a reflection of a person. A *reflection* of me. It was only a reflection. The real me was right here inside my body watching a reflection in a mirror. Had I finally found me? The real me?

I yanked the offensive white eyelash out.

Look at me, I accomplished something. And I was real. I was Evie.

I *am* Evie.

Afterword

I F SOMEONE IS HURTING YOU, say something. It doesn't matter how old you are. It isn't right. You are a human being and deserve love and respect just like everyone else does. I can say those words now but when I was a child, I couldn't even imagine doing something that might "fix" my life.

Deep down, you might believe, if only I try harder, maybe it won't be so bad, maybe the abuse will stop. It won't. It won't stop until either you get away from the abuser, or the abuser gets caught abusing you. You need to tell. If you don't, the abuser will eat you alive from the inside out. No matter how much you comply, it will never be enough. They will always want more.

Even if the abuse happened years ago and you "got away," I still encourage you to get help. Right now. Not tomorrow. Today. Even if you don't think it's affecting you, it will at some point down the road. It's better to be prepared than have the monster jump out of nowhere to mess up your life and destroy your health, essentially kill you. Learn how to control the monster instead of letting the monster control you. Enough is enough!

CN
March 2022

References

https://www.clinmedjournals.org/articles/jfmdp/journal-of-family-medicine-and-disease-prevention-jfmdp-3-059.php?jid=jfmdp

https://www.choosingtherapy.com/raised-by-narcissists/

https://www.teach-through-love.com/types-of-emotional-abuse.html

https://kidshealth.org/en/kids/handle-abuse.html

https://endingviolencecanada.org/getting-help/

Acknowledgements

PROFOUND THANKS GO TO THOSE doctors, psychologists and college professors who helped me find the real me; to the members of various mental-health groups who shared their stories over the years and listened to mine; and to those I worked with and counseled, you who asked me to help you. Without you, I would still be held captive in the mental basement of my childhood fears and confusion.

About the Author

CATINA NOBLE IS AN OTTAWA writer with over two hundred publications including books, articles, short stories and poetry. Her work has appeared in many publications including *Woman's World Magazine, Chicken Soup for the Soul, Bywords, Riverview Park Review, PEN, YTravel Blog, The Mindful Word, Mojito Mother*, and *Baby Post*. Her poem "You Can't See Me" took first place in the Canadian Authors Association's National Capital Writing Contest in 2014. Three of her books have received the Reader's Favorite Five Star award: *Vacancy at the Food Court & Other Short Stories*; *I'm Glad I Didn't Kill Myself*; and *Everest Base Camp: Close Call*. In 2006, Catina graduated from Algonquin College with her Social Services Worker Diploma and in 2009, she graduated from Carleton University with a Bachelor's Degree in Psychology. She works full time in her field, writes, and is currently enrolled in the Addictions & Mental Health Program at Algonquin College.

Books by Catina Noble

El Camino on a Wrecked Ankle (non-fiction)
Everest Base Camp: Close Call (non-fiction)
Vacancy at the Food Court & Other Short Stories (fiction)
Not Just Me (fiction, Part 1 of the Teal Trilogy)
Not Again (fiction, Part 2 of the Teal Trilogy)
This is It (fiction, Part 3 of the Teal Trilogy)
Lost at 13 (non-fiction)
I'm Glad I Didn't Kill Myself (non-fiction)
Katzenjammer (poetry)

Available in print or digital from the Amazon dots.